This book is dedicated to my family and supporters.

Thank you so much for all of your Love & Encouragement!

- **Love Erica**

Chapter 1

Khi's mind churned like a storm as he sped down the highway, tightly gripping the steering wheel. The night stretched endlessly before him, with the headlights of Nicole's car glowing faintly in his rearview mirror. He didn't know where he was going, only that Trinity couldn't be at the house when Xanae woke up.

He felt bad for leaving, but he didn't have a choice. Xanae had been desperate to tell him something, and he had left her, abandoned her in her moment of need. His stomach twisted as he thought of her, fragile yet strong, waiting for him while he tore off into the night with more questions than answers.

As much as he hated to admit it, this wasn't about Xanae. Not entirely. Trinity's fate hovered over him like a dark shadow, tangled in a web of mystery that he couldn't ignore.

The thought of losing her without closure ate away at him. Even now, Khi was blind to the truth, clueless that the woman bleeding out in his back seat wasn't his sister at all. He caught a glimpse of her through the rearview mirror, pale and motionless, and the sight spurred him to action. With a sharp yank of the wheel, he veered onto the next exit, tires screeching against the asphalt.

Fifteen minutes later, the cars pulled to a stop in front of an estate that seemed to be ripped straight from the pages of a dream. There were tall iron gates and meticulously trimmed rose bushes that released a sweet perfume into the cool night air. Beyond the gates, there was a stone pathway that led to a marble fountain that gushed crystal-clear water in mesmerizing cascades.

Nicole gasped as she stepped out of her car, she had never seen anything like this before. The estate was regal, but the urgency of the situation snapped her back to reality. She hurried to the back seat of Khi's car, inhaling deeply while trying to control her shaking hands as she checked Trinity's pulse.

"Where are we Khi? We have to get her to a hospital. Her pulse is getting weaker by the second." Nicole urged.

"No hospitals!" Khi barked, slamming the car door behind him. He paced for a moment, running a hand through his locs, then stared Nicole straight in the eyes. He needed her to understand him clearly.

"This is my new crib. She stays here until she's better. No hospitals! Didn't you go to school for this shit? I'll pay you double; I'll make it 7,000 a week. Just do whatever it takes to make sure she stays alive." Khi instructed.

Nicole stared back at him, stunned, but Khi didn't wait for a reply.

"Stay here, I'll open the door and come back to carry her inside" he said, already heading toward the house.

Khi sprinted towards the front door, breathing rapidly as he fumbled for the keys. This estate was supposed to be a sanctuary, a fresh start, a place where he and Xanae could dream about their future without ghosts of the past haunting every corner. He knew that he would never be able to peacefully lay his head in a home where his mother took her last breath, so he immediately started looking for a new house.

It had only been a week since he purchased the home, reaching out to the same realtor who had helped him secure his commercial property. He had planned to surprise Xanae with an engagement party here, imagining her face lighting up as she stepped through the doors. But life had a way of twisting dreams into nightmares.

He knew that he couldn't take Trinity to a hotel where questions would follow them like blood trails, and hospitals weren't an option, there were too many eyes, too many prying hands. Reluctantly, he had decided to bring her to what should have been his and Xanae's refuge.

After unlocking the door and scanning the house for any signs of trouble Khi rushed back outside. The night was still, but his pulse raced as he approached Nicole. Trinity was sprawled across the backseat, her face was contorted, and blood stained her clothes. Khi swallowed hard, pushing down the knot of guilt and confusion threatening to choke him. Gently, he lifted her into his arms, careful not to jostle her fragile body.

He quickly carried Trinity up the stone path. Every detail of the mansion mocked him now. The luxury, the perfection, the dreams he had woven into its walls. All of it felt pointless.

Inside the estate, the air was cool and sterile, the pristine white floors shimmered under crystal chandeliers. The bedroom he chose was the only fully furnished room in the house and it had an attached bathroom. The rich scent of fresh-cut flowers clashing with the metallic tang of the blood spilling out of Trinity threatened to gag him.

He laid her on the bed and stood over her for a moment watching her chest rise and fall, each shallow breath a reminder of how close she was to the edge.

Nicole entered the room, her presence pulling Khi out of his thoughts. Her eyes darted between him and Trinity as she sat her medical bag on the bed. Her movements were swift and precise as she worked to stabilize her.

Khi hovered nearby, his fists clenched. The house seemed to close in around him, every tick of the clock felt like a countdown to something he couldn't stop. He had so many questions and couldn't shake the underlying fear of what could be.

As he watched Nicole work a cold determination settled over him. No matter what it took, he would get answers. No matter what happened, he wouldn't let Trinity die.

"How long do you think she will be out?" Khi asked, his voice rough.

Nicole sighed, pulling out her stethoscope and blood pressure cuff.

"It's hard to say. She lost a lot of blood. It could be hours, days, even months. Her body is in shock, only time will tell."

Nicole wasn't telling him what he needed to hear. He needed Trinity to wake up, he needed to hear her side of the story.

"Clean her up. Get her out of these bloody-ass clothes" he said sharply, his tone more commanding than he intended. He softened slightly, his eyes meeting Nicole's.

"I need you here Twenty-four-seven. If there's any change make sure you call me, I don't care what time it is. I need to know the second she wakes up." Khi instructed.

Nicole nodded, her hands already moving to check Trinity's vitals. "Got it. I will take good care of her Khi. You don't need to worry." She assured.

“I’ll have Noriega drop off groceries. The cable is already on, and the security code is 8181. Remember I said no phones! Take this throwaway and only use it to call me, Khi instructed, handing her a flip phone. He started for the door but paused, turning back. “Don’t tell anyone you’re here, and don’t leave her side.”

“Yes Khi. Understood, is there anything else you need me to do for you?” Nicole replied with a smile. She didn’t mind the intensity of his demands, especially not with the money he was offering. Seven grand a week was more than she had ever dreamed of making at the hospital as a LPN. Then there was Khi himself: the way he moved, the power he exuded, his neatly twisted locs, chocolate skin and raspy voice all made her panties moist. Standing in his luxurious home only confirmed what she had always suspected. Khi wasn’t just selling drugs, he was a kingpin, moving weight like few others in their city. She was more than willing to oblige any of his requests.

Khi stood in place for a moment, his eyes traveled down Nicole's curvaceous frame. He noticed the way her mint green scrubs hugged her hips and ass. She was sexy, but there was nothing he wanted from her other than her medical expertise. Without a response he turned and left, his footsteps echoing through the house.

When Khi stepped outside, he inhaled deeply, the cool air doing little to ease the turmoil inside him. He climbed into his car and pulled away, watching the mansion growing smaller in his rearview mirror. The life he had so carefully built was unraveling, and he didn't know how to stop it.

■■

The drive back to the old house was a blur. The harder he tried to piece together what happened, the foggier the picture became. He drove stoically, each mile feeling like a futile escape from the chaos consuming his life.

When he arrived, the house was dark except for the light from a small lamp in the living room. Rock sat in an armchair across from Xanae, his eyes locked on her as if he were guarding her or coveting her.

Khi felt a twinge of unease as he walked towards them.

“Damn, she still ain’t up?” He asked, as he approached the couch. He leaned down, pressing his lips softly against Xanae’s forehead. Her face was bruised, leaving evidence of the tussle with Trinity, but she was still beautiful and serene.

"Nah," Rock replied, standing abruptly. His movements were rigid, as if he suddenly felt uncomfortable. "She might have hit her head, ain't no telling when she will wake up."

There was something in Rock's tone, an edge that Khi couldn't quite place. Normally, he would've picked up on it, he would have clearly saw the jealousy simmering just beneath the surface, the barely veiled resentment. But tonight, Khi's mind was too clouded to really notice.

"You sure you don't know what happened? Why were they fighting over the gun?" Khi asked, pacing the room. "None of this shit is adding up."

Rock shrugged, keeping his expression carefully blank. "I don't know. I just did what I had to do. I guess we have to wait for one of them to wake up and fill in the blanks to get the full story."

His words were cold, detached, and they rubbed Khi the wrong way. But before he could press further, Rock added-

"Look, I'm heading out. Shiyah's got the baby, and you know she's solid. Just focus on handling your business here. I'll hold things down at the store."

"Appreciate it fam. Tell Shiyah I'll check on KJ in a few." Khi said, clasping Rock's hand briefly.

"Will do" Rock replied before heading out.

Khi turned back to Xanae, his heart aching at the sight of her. He sat beside her and held her hand as he whispered in her ear.

"Baby, I'm so sorry. Please wake up. I need you. I'll fix this. I swear I'll make it right. Just wake up."

Hours passed as he poured out his regrets, his promises, his fears while Xanae slept silently. At some point exhaustion took over, pulling him into a restless sleep on the edge of the couch.

"Khi... Khi, where's the baby?"

The faint sound of Xanae's voiced snatched him from his slumber. Relief flooded him as he quickly sat up and reached for her, cupping her face and planting kisses on her lips and cheeks.

"Damn baby, I'm so glad you're up," he breathed, his voice thick with emotion. "Are you okay?"

"Where's the baby?" Xanae repeated. "What happened? Why does your face look like that?" She asked. Her throat was dry, and pain radiated through her entire body with every movement. Her eyes desperately searched his as she held her breath waiting on a response.

"He's safe," Khi reassured her quickly. "Shiyah took him for the night. Don't worry about my face, I'm cool. Just tell me what happened today."

Xanae breathed a sigh of relief knowing that KJ was in good hands but hesitated before responding to Khi. She knew that the truth would destroy him, but he deserved to know. She could see the worry etched into his face, the emotions he was fighting to hold back. She took a deep breath, bracing herself for what she was about to say.

"Khi........ Trinity is not your sister. I found your mom's journal. She wrote about everything, about Harmony, about the group home. Trinity was one of the foster kids. She killed the foster parents; she killed Harmony, and she forced Kay to help her hide the bodies" Xanae said softly.

Her words felt like daggers as the details spilled out of her. Khi's body went rigid as the truth slammed into him.

"What the hell are you talking about Nae?" He asked in confusion.

Xanae held his gaze, her eyes glistening with unshed tears. "She's not your sister Khi, she's a liar, a manipulator. She's a Serial Killer." Xanae cried.

The room fell into a suffocating silence as the revelation escaped her lips.

Xanae's voice quivered with urgency as she tried to piece together the right words to make Khi understand.

"Khi, I read Kay's journal. It's all there. She killed Harmony and your mother helped her move the body. I confronted her about it - Why do you think she attacked me?!" Xanae explained.

Khi frowned, his brows pulling together in disbelief as he rubbed the back of his neck, pacing the room.

"Nae, listen to yourself. What you're saying doesn't even make sense. Ma? She wouldn't do something like that, and even if she did, why would she write it all down? It's probably something she made up to cope, you know? She told me she used to write short stories when she was in rehab, stuff to escape her thoughts." Khi reasoned.

He reached out for Xanae, gently rubbing her face as he tried to kiss her, as if to pacify her concerns. But Xanae pulled away sharply. Her voice rose, refusing to back down.

"No Khi. Stop dismissing me! I know this is hard for you to hear, but it is the truth. I am not making this up. I saw it in her handwriting, with my own two eyes. Every detail. Every word. Why won't you just listen to me?" Xanae pleaded.

The air felt charged with unspoken fears and buried truths. Khi stared at her, as he tried to process what she was telling him.

"Nae... I'm not saying I don't believe you, but you telling me that Trinity is some killer pretending to be my sister. You think I wouldn't have figured that out by now? I know my sister, I would know if something was off." Khi insisted.

Xanae let out a bitter laugh, she couldn't believe that Khi thought that she was lying after everything that Trinity had done.

"Would you Khi? Would you really? Or are you so desperate to have Harmony back that you're blind to the truth that's right in front of you?" Xanae questioned.

Her words cut deep, but Khi didn't flinch. Instead, he looked toward the window and exhaled before responding.

"You don't get it Nae. I've been searching for her my whole life. I gave up damn near everything to find her, and now you're telling me that it was all for nothing? That she's gone, and this... this stranger came in and played me? I don't know if I *can* believe that Ma. Khi replied solemnly.

Xanae shook her head, her voice softening but no less insistent.

"I do get it Khi, I really do. You wanted to find her so bad that you didn't even question it when Trinity showed up. But something is not right, you have to see that."

Khi turned to her and squinted his eyes. "So what? I just accept this and move on? How can I trust any of this? What if you're wrong Nae?"

Her voice rose again, a desperate edge creeping into her tone.

"I'm not wrong! Did you even ask her anything about your past? Anything only Harmony would know? Did you?" Xanae questioned.

Khi hesitated, and Xanae saw the moment of doubt in his eyes. It was enough to make her push harder.

"See? You didn't. You wanted so bad for it to be real that you didn't stop to think about how it all lined up. Trinity came out of nowhere Khi. Look at what's happened since she got here. Everything has fallen apart, and now you're standing here, defending her! She took my best friend! She took everything Khi! Xanae cried.

"I don't want to argue with you Nae. You've been through enough. I just need you to trust me. I'm going to figure this out, I promise."

Xanae stared at him, her heart heavy with disappointment. "You want me to trust you, but you can't even believe me. You can't trust that I'm telling you the truth!"

Khi sighed as he ran his hand down his face. He grabbed a bottle of water, and some pain medicine, handing them to Xanae.

"Please Nae, just rest. Let me handle this." Khi pleaded.

Xanae's shoulders sagged, she was exhausted, and her entire body was sore. She knew this wasn't the time to push further, even though every fiber of her being wanted to scream at him to believe her. Reluctantly, she took the pills, swallowing them with a sip of water, as Khi turned to leave.

"The journal is upstairs. If you don't believe me, read it yourself. Then we'll see if you still think this is just some story your mom made up."

Khi paused but didn't turn back to her. He stood there for a moment, his body tense, before walking toward the stairs. Xanae watched him go. She wanted to believe he would see the truth, but deep down she feared he was too far gone, clinging to a dream that had already turned into a nightmare.

Khi climbed the stairs, his mind racing as he searched for the journal. He rifled through their bedroom, checking drawers and closets, then moved to the hallways and spare rooms, opening cabinets and pulling back furniture. Nothing. His frustration grew with every passing moment. Finally, after what felt like an eternity, he gave up and headed back downstairs.

Xanae sat on the couch, her body stiff with anticipation. She turned her head slightly as Khi sank into the cushion beside her.

“So? Did you read it?” she asked.

Khi exhaled heavily, rubbing his palms against his thighs before stroking a hand through her hair in an attempt to soothe her. “No. I looked everywhere, but I couldn’t find it.”

“What do you mean, you couldn’t find it? It was here Khi! I brought it in the house with me after I got home from the spa! That crazy bitch must’ve taken it with her! Where is she?” Xanae demanded.

Khi hesitated, the truth hovering on the tip of his tongue. He knew Xanae wasn't ready for it, not now, not with her wounds fresh and her emotions raw. Instead, he lied.

"She's dead Nae," he said quietly.

The color drained from Xanae's face. She blinked at him, as if her mind couldn't digest what she had just heard.

"She's dead? How?" She replied trying to remember the events that had transpired earlier.

Khi leaned forward, resting his elbows on his knees. His head hung low for a moment before he forced himself to look at her.

"Rock told me what happened. He said he walked in and saw y'all struggling over the gun. He shot her, and by the time I got here it was too late... she was already gone." Khi lied.

"I had the crew handle the body. She's gone Nae. You don't have to worry about her anymore."

Xanae stared at him in shock. She tried to form a response but couldn't bring herself to speak. All she could mutter was- "Rock saved my life?"

She should have felt relief, but instead, a complicated mix of emotions swirled within her. Trinity was gone. The person who had brought chaos and danger into their lives was no longer a threat. But the journal, the secrets, the lies, were all like a splinter she couldn't remove.

"Baby, I know this is a lot. I know how much you wanted her to be your sister, but I need you to listen to me." She said softly, reaching for Khi's hand. "That journal was real Khi. I am not making this up. She wasn't Harmony. She wasn't your sister."

Khi's jaw tightened, he could hear the conviction in her voice, but his heart wasn't ready to accept it. He had spent years imagining the day he would reunite with Harmony. To have that dream snatched away now felt unbearable.

"Nae, none of that matters now. She's gone. Let's just leave it alone." he said finally.

Xanae shook her head in frustration. She could hear the doubt and resentment in his tone.

"How can you just brush this off? How can you not want to know the truth?" She asked.

"I'll find out the truth when the time is right." Khi replied.

Xanae didn't know what his words meant, but she didn't argue. Instead, she took a deep breath and shifted the conversation.

"Khi... I just want all of this to be over. We can't keep living like this. We have a son, and he can't grow up in this kind of mess." Her voice softened, her eyes pleading with him. "Whatever beef you have with Dame, you need to let it go. I don't care about the money! I love you and I will be with you no matter what, but you have to leave this life behind."

Khi's expression turned cold. "You don't have to worry about Dame either Nae," he said firmly.

Her stomach twisted. Something in his tone made her uneasy. "What do you mean I don't have to worry? Khi, what did you do?"

"It's handled" he said simply, void of any emotion.

Xanae could hear her heart pounding in her ears. "Khi what does 'handled' mean?" she pressed, her breathing increasing.

Khi turned to face her, "It means it's done Xanae. That's all you need to know."

She stared at him, now realizing what he meant. He had killed Dame. She didn't need him to spell it out.

Trinity was gone; Dame was gone, she could finally wake up from the bad dream that had become their lives. She felt free for a split second before doubt crept in and whispered that the nightmare wasn't over. It was just beginning.

Chapter 2

Nicole flipped through the endless sea of channels on the 70-inch TV mounted on the wall of the spacious living room. The house, with its marble floors and grand chandeliers felt more like a gilded prison than a dream vacation at a Luxury Airbnb. She had been caring for Trinity for an agonizing week now, and still Trinity hadn't stirred. Outside of reality TV shows, the highlight of her day was Khi's calls. He checked in every hour like clockwork, his voice always a mixture of hope and worry as he asked the same question: "Any change?" And every time, Nicole delivered the same answer: "No."

Loneliness chipped away at her, and boredom crawled under her skin. The quiet house, while beautiful, still felt suffocating. Khi's warning echoed in her mind- *Don't let anyone know where you are!* She was trying hard to adhere to his rules, but isolation was pushing her to the brink.

She dropped the remote on the couch with a sigh and picked up the throwaway phone Khi had given her. She thought about sneaking a friend over for some company, just for a little while. She entered her sister's number, and her finger hovered over the call button for a split second before the sound of faint coughing made her freeze.

Her head whipped toward the hallway as the coughing grew louder. Heart pounding, Nicole bolted toward the bedroom where Trinity lay.

Trinity's eyes fluttered open, glassy and confused, as her lips parted to speak.

"Who... who are you? Where am I?" She asked. Her voice was raspy, her words barely audible.

Nicole rushed to her side, adjusting the pillows behind her and brushing strands of hair from her damp forehead.

"I'm Nicole," she said gently. "You're safe. I know you must be starving, and you probably need pain meds too. Let me take care of you." Nicole offered.

Trinity struggled to sit up, her limbs were weak and if felt as if they no longer obeyed her commands. "How did I get here?" she croaked, her throat raw and sore.

Nicole hesitated for a moment before explaining.

"Khi brought you here after... after you got shot. I'm a Nurse, he hired me to help you recover." She stuttered. Khi hadn't told her what to tell Trinity when she woke up, but she had to offer her some type of explanation.

She retrieved her stethoscope from her bag and began checking Trinity's vitals.

Trinity's heart sank at Nicole's words. *Khi brought me here? Why? Did Xanae tell him what she found in Kay's journal? Does he know?* Her mind raced with questions, but she kept her face neutral as panic crept in.

"Where is Khi?" she asked cautiously.

Nicole gave her a small smile. “I was just about to call him. He’s been waiting for you to wake up.”

“No!” Trinity blurted, her voice louder now. She grabbed Nicole’s wrist, her grip surprisingly strong for someone so weak. “Please, don’t call him yet. I… I don’t want him to see me like this.”

Nicole blinked in confusion. “But he told me to call as soon as you woke up. He’s been so worried about you.”

“I know,” Trinity said, softening her tone. “I just… Please. At least let me take a shower and get dressed first. I don’t want him to see me like this. Just give me a little time, okay?”

Nicole studied her face, seeing the desperation there, and reluctantly nodded. “Okay. I’ll help you get cleaned up first. Then I’ll call him.”

“Thank you.” Trinity breathed, relief flooding her voice.

Nicole helped Trinity out of bed, guiding her fragile body toward the bathroom. Inside, the massive whirlpool tub gleamed under the bathroom's soft lighting. Nicole leaned over the edge, filling the tub with warm water and pouring in fragrant bubble bath. The scent of lavender filled the air, but Trinity barely noticed. Her mind was racing. She had to get out of there before Nicole called Khi. She couldn't let him see her, not yet, not like this. She needed time to think, she had to get away.

The sound of the water was a low roar in her ears as she weighed her options. Then it hit her! There was only one way out. That familiar burning sensation coursed through her body, the one she had tried so hard to suppress to no avail. She knew what she had to do. She had to buy herself sometime.

Without warning, Trinity lunged forward. Her body collided with Nicole's, sending them both crashing against the porcelain wall. Nicole gasped; her eyes wide with shock as her head slammed into the hard surface. Before she could react, Trinity was on her, using every ounce of strength she had left to push Nicole into the tub. Water splashed everywhere, drenching the floor and soaking their clothes.

Nicole thrashed, dazed and panicked, her arms flailing as she tried to push Trinity off. But Trinity held firm, her fingers gripping the back of Nicole's head as she forced it under the water. Bubbles erupted from Nicole's mouth as she struggled, but her movements grew weaker with every passing second. Finally, she stopped moving, and the water settled into an eerie calm.

Trinity tried to catch her breath as she slowly released her grip and climbed out of the tub, her wounded body screaming in protest. Pain radiated through where the bullet had torn into her torso and came out her side, but she knew she couldn't rest. She didn't have time to waste, she had to move.

She staggered through the house, searching for Nicole's belongings. She spotted a purse in the living room and rummaged through it. Her fingers closed around a wallet, a fat envelope stuffed with cash, and a set of car keys. Relief washed over her, she had what she needed.

Trinity moved quickly, grabbing the bag of medical supplies from the bedroom. Her mind was clearer now, all she was focused on was survival.

Without a second thought, she headed to the front door. When she stepped into the crisp evening air, the cool breeze bit against her damp skin. She noticed Nicole's car parked neatly in the driveway, a shining beacon of her escape. Moving quickly, she slid into the driver's seat, her hands shaking as she gripped the wheel. The car roared to life with the twist of the key, and after scanning her surroundings for any sign of danger, she sped off into the night.

Every mile she put between herself and that house felt like a small victory, but loneliness consumed her as she thought about what would come next. The people she had once leaned on were all gone. There was no Dame, KJ, or Khi. Her worst fear had come to pass, she was utterly and completely alone. In her mind the blame landed squarely on Xanae. That bitch had ruined everything, and Trinity vowed that she wouldn't leave Georgia for good. She just needed time to regroup. When she returned, Xanae would feel every ounce of the anguish that burned in her chest.

Khi listened to a repetitive set of rings that eventually forwarded to Nicole's voicemail for the fourth time. He grew more and more frustrated each time Nicole didn't pick up the phone. She always answered, especially when it came to updates about Trinity. He slid the phone into his pocket and grabbed his keys, shaking his head. Something wasn't right.

"Baby, I gotta handle something. I'll be back" he said, his voice gruff as he headed toward the front door.

From the couch, Xanae crossed her arms and glared at him.

"Where are you going now Khi?" she demanded.

Over the past week, his unexplained absences had grown more frequent, leaving Xanae feeling sidelined and unimportant. She couldn't shake the feeling that he was lying to her, or worse, prioritizing the game over their relationship to cope with his losses and demons.

Khi sighed, leaning down to kiss her forehead. "I gotta handle some shit with Rock. I'll be back later."

But Xanae wasn't buying it. She could sense that there was something he wasn't telling her, and she felt as if he resented her for what she had revealed about Trinity.

"Khi, she's dead! Trinity was just some psycho bitch who finessed us all and made you believe she was your sister! Why can't you see that?" Xanae questioned, staring at him with pleading eyes.

He didn't answer her. He just repeated himself with an edge of finality. "I'll be back, Nae."

The door closed behind him, leaving Xanae seething. He was acting different. She hated how Trinity's ghost lingered between them, pulling Khi away from her time and time again. The worst part was the journal was still missing. Deep down, Xanae knew that Khi might never fully believe her.

Twenty minutes later, Khi pulled up to the house where he had stashed Trinity. He immediately noticed that Nicole's car wasn't parked in the driveway. He stepped inside cautiously, peeking around each corner, his Givenchy boots echoing behind him. When he saw the wet floor in the hallway, his heart began to race, dread curling in his gut.

He slowly approached the bathroom, his hand instinctively reaching for the 9mm tucked in his waistband.

The faint sound of running water greeted him as he pushed the door open. A lump the size of a baseball formed in his throat when he saw Nicole's lifeless body floating in the tub. He could tell she was dead by her lifeless eyes staring at the ceiling

His stomach dropped as the truth crashed down on him, Xanae had been right all along. Trinity was no victim. She was a danger; a predator, a liar, and she had been playing him the entire time. Finessing at its finest.

He let out a sharp curse, his hands shaking as he turned off the water. Pulling his phone from his pocket, he dialed Rock.

"Yo," Rock answered on the first ring.

"I need a crew, send them to my new crib, I'm texting you the address. You ain't gonna believe this shit Man. Xanae was right after all. We gotta find that bitch Trinity before she does something crazy." Khi explained.

"On it ASAP, fam." Rock replied, not asking any questions.

After they hung up Khi sent the address, the sick smell of death floated in the air causing him to wait inside his car.

He leaned back in the driver's seat and closed his eyes, rubbing his temples as he tried to figure out where Trinity could've gone. He had to find her; he couldn't let her hurt anyone else. His mind filled with anger and shame; Trinity had fooled him completely. She had been in his home, near his woman, his son, his mother. Now she was loose, a dangerous wildcard that could come back and wreak havoc at any time. Until she was found, Xanae and everyone else he cared about were in jeopardy.

Suddenly a shadow moved behind him. Khi's instincts screamed too late. A pair of hands shot forward, wrapping tightly around his throat. His eyes flew open, and he struggled to breathe, clawing at the grip that was cutting off his air supply. He reached for his pistol, but two quick punches landed against the side of his face, dazing him. The world spun as a thick bag was pulled over his head, and he felt himself being yanked out of the car. His body hit the ground with a heavy thud before being dragged roughly toward the trunk of another vehicle.

Disoriented and furious, Khi tried to fight back, but his assailants were fast and strong. The last thing he heard before the trunk slammed shut was the muffled sound of an engine starting.

The house was eerily quiet as Rock and Noriega stepped inside. Rock glanced around cautiously.

"His truck is still here, he ain't go too far." he muttered, trying to ignore the uneasiness building in his chest.

Noriega looked skeptical as he scanned the perimeter. "Didn't you say he was gonna be here waiting on us?"

"Yeah" Rock replied. "This don't feel right. Let's check inside."

The two men quietly moved deeper into the house, splitting up, working the first and second floors with practiced efficiency.

A shout from down the hall shattered the silence.

“Yo, come in here!” Noriega bellowed, his voice echoing with urgency. Rock hurried toward the bathroom, where Noriega stood in the doorway.

“Shit!” Rock hissed when he saw Nicole’s body floating in the tub, blood had mixed with the water, tinting it a muted pink color.

“That’s the chick he hired to take care of his sister, ain’t it?” Noriega said, shaking his head.

“Yeah,” Rock replied grimly. “What the fuck happened to her?”

Noriega didn’t have an answer, he refocused on the job at hand.

“This is why he called us here, ain’t no other explanation. Let’s get to it.” He said, turning to the two street soldiers they had brought along, who had been guarding the outside of the house until they heard Noriega's call.

"Y'all start cleaning this up, make sure it's spotless. Nobody needs to know what went down here." Noriega directed.

The soldiers nodded, immediately setting to work as Rock pulled out his phone and dialed Khi's number. He pressed the phone to his ear, his foot tapping impatiently against the floor. Once again it went straight to voicemail. Frowning, he tried again and again. Each time, the call dropped to voicemail quicker than the last.

"I don't know where the hell this nigga went. He ain't answering, but he gotta show up eventually. Just finish cleaning this shit up." Rock mumbled in frustration as he shoved the phone back into his pocket.

As the soldiers scrubbed the blood-streaked tub and packed Nicole's lifeless body into a black bag, Rock and Noriega exchanged a glance. Both men knew something wasn't adding up.

"Whatever's going on, I got a feeling this shit ain't gonna end clean." Noriega said, his voice low.

Rock nodded grimly. He had the same feeling, and it wasn't a good one.

Chapter 3

Xanae rocked back and forth, wrapping her arms tightly around herself as if trying to hold her crumbling world together. Hot tears streamed down her face; it had been 3 days. Three endless, soul-crushing days had passed since Khi disappeared.

The silence of his absence was louder than any scream, and it clawed at her sanity. She replayed their last conversation over and over, her words sharp as broken glass cutting into her heart. If only she could take them back. If only she had stopped to consider how he felt, the war he was fighting, the guilt he carried for not being there to protect her and the agony of losing his mother again, this time to the very drug that had stolen her from his childhood.

"God please. Please, just let him be okay." Xanae whispered, her voice shaking as she gazed upward.

Her prayer broke into a sob, her body folding under the weight of her anguish. The sound of the doorbell shattered her solitude, and her heart leapt with desperate hope. She bolted down the stairs, her feet barely touching the ground, and flung open the door without hesitation.

Standing there, with a bag of food in one hand and a bottle of wine in the other, was Rock.

"Rock?" What are you doing here?" She said with a mix of surprise and disappointment.

Rock's expression softened as he took in her tear-streaked face, her swollen eyes a testament to sleepless nights.

"I know you going through it Nae. I just wanted to check on you and lil' man, I brought you some food and something to help you relax." He said as he held up the bag and bottle.

Xanae wiped her face with both hands, her exhaustion evident. "I appreciate it Rock, but I don't have much of an appetite and KJ is upstairs sleeping."

Rock stepped inside without waiting for an invitation, his presence filling the room like an intruder.

"I get it, but you gotta take care of yourself. I know Khi would want that. So just try to eat a little, okay? For me. If it were Shiyah, I would expect Khi to do the same." Rock lied. The truth was he was glad Khi was missing, and he was going to take every chance he could to get closer to Xanae.

Xanae pressed her lips together in hesitation, but she reluctantly nodded and moved to the couch, sinking into her favorite spot.

Rock disappeared into the kitchen and returned a few minutes later with a plate of rice, chicken, broccoli, and a spring roll, along with a glass of chilled Chardonnay.

"Thanks." Xanae said genuinely, but the plate might as well have been filled with stones. She picked up a piece of broccoli, pushing it around as her thoughts ran rampant.

"I just don't understand it Rock, none of this makes sense. Why would he leave without a word? I can't stop thinking... what if he's dead? What if someone in Dame's crew retaliated? What if I never see him again?" She cried.

"He's good shawty. We handled that shit with Dame already." Rock replied.

"You don't know that for sure Rock! I can't just sit here and wait, tomorrow I'm filing a missing person report!"

Rock shifted uncomfortably, then took a deep breath. "I talked to him."

Hope sparked in Xanae's soul, and she immediately turned to face Rock. "You did? When? Why didn't he call me?" She asked anxiously.

"He just needed to get away for a while to clear his head, he told me to look out for you, and to let you know he's okay." Rock said, resting his hand on her shoulder.

Her eyes searched his face, desperate for answers that eluded her.

"That doesn't make sense Rock. He wouldn't just leave us, not like this." Xanae replied in disbelief.

"He just needs .... some time to figure some shit out shawty, just chill." Rock replied. His hesitation was apparent, but he had already lied so there was no point in stopping now.

"Time to figure it out? Figure out what?! I needed him! After everything I've been through... I needed him here. With me. With KJ." Xanae yelled as she pointed at her chest.

Rock exhaled heavily, before slightly tightening his grip on her shoulder. "I know Nae. I get it, but you gotta keep it together, for KJ if nothing else. I'm here. Whatever you need, I got you."

Xanae's chest heaved as she used every effort to hold back the tears threatening to spill again. She shook her head and stood. "I can't do this. I need to talk to him. I need to hear it from him directly, not through you. I need you to leave." She said, staring Rock dead in the eyes. She felt like he knew something that he wasn't telling her, and she couldn't deal with the Bros over hoes shit right now.

Rock, wanted to protest but instead he gave a slow nod.

"Alright, I'll head out. But don't hesitate to call me if you need anything, okay?" He offered again.

Xanae didn't answer, instead she silently walked him to the door. As he stepped out, he turned back to look at her. "Take care of yourself Nae."

She closed the door and leaned against it, her legs buckling beneath her. She didn't notice the way Rock's steps faltered on the path; his shoulders heavy with a secret he hadn't dared to share. If Xanae knew what he knew about the bloodied body in the bathroom and the abandoned truck with no trace of Khi, she would never forgive him. He didn't know where Khi was, and he didn't care. In his mind this was a new beginning. A chance to take everything Khi had built and make it his own. If things went his way Xanae would stand by his side, a Queen to his kingdom, while Khi faded into nothing more than a distant memory.

Khi's head throbbed, each pulse felt like a hammer striking against the fragile wall of his consciousness. His mouth was dry, his tongue thick and cracked as though it was coated in sand. Shackled to a chair in a stifling, lightless room, the days bled together in a cycle of fog, hunger and humiliation.

His stomach twisted in sharp, relentless pain, and the rank stench of his soiled clothes was torment. He racked his brain over and over, desperate to figure out who had orchestrated this nightmare. Dame was his only adversary that had presented himself, but Khi knew that in the Drug Game there were enemies lurking behind every corner. The question still remained- Who the hell was behind this?

He cursed under his breath. *Caught slipping, like a damn rookie.* He thought, promising himself that if he made it out of this alive, he would never let it happen again.

Footsteps echoed from beyond the thick door, each step rattling his frayed nerves. Khi straightened, forcing himself to breathe slow and steady despite the adrenaline flooding his veins. The door groaned open, and a burst of harsh light filled the small room. Khi winced, his eyes burning as they adjusted. A towering figure stepped into view; his silhouette framed by the blinding glare.

“Malakhi Banks, do you know why ya here?” the man said, his voice a deep rumble laced with menace.

Khi blinked away the haze, locking eyes with his captor. He was a stocky man with a hard jaw and a thick Jamaican accent.

"Nah Mutha Fucka, but I'm guessing you about to tell me." Khi retorted, his voice hoarse but lined in defiance.

The man smirked, his gold tooth catching the light. "Ya owe me two million dollars, and me want it today, or ya won't make it back to that pretty likkle girlfriend of yours in Georgia. Ya undastand?" he said coldly.

Khi's stomach flipped, but his expression didn't waver.

"I don't owe you shit," he snapped, despite the fear biting at the edges of his nerves. "I don't even know you, fuck the money and the circumstances- DON'T speak on her!"

The man was Biggs, as Khi would later learn. Khi's eyes followed him as he leaned in so close their noses touched.

"Big balls, huh?" he said, his voice almost amused. "But big balls can get a man killed. You nah know me personally, but ya had dealings wit' Dame, yeah?" Biggs questioned.

"What does my business with Dame have to do with you?" Khi spat.

Biggs' grin disappeared, replaced by a cold stare.

"Everyting! Dame owed me two million. He was supposed to pay me back once he recovered what ya stole from him."

"I didn't steal shit from Dame," Khi retorted.

Biggs ignored him, continuing as though he hadn't heard. "I had eyes on him for weeks. Followed him to some house, but funny ting... nobody ever see him come out. Where he dea? Hmm?" Biggs said as he leaned closer, his voice dropping to a near whisper. "He nah vanish pon thin air."

A pit formed in his gut when Khi realized who the man was. Biggs wasn't just some low-level thug. He was

Dame's connect; he was the big fish and now Khi was tangled in his net. He took a slow breath, forcing himself to think clearly. Biggs was dangerous, no doubt about it. But predators like him thrived on fear. Showing weakness would only dig his grave deeper.

"That's neither here nor there," Khi said finally, leaning back in the chair with as much composure as his restraints allowed. "I ain't giving you two mil. Your beef was with Dame, not me, but I can make you a deal that will make you more than what Dame owed you." Khi said, thinking quickly.

Biggs was a lover of money, so he was immediately intrigued by Khi's offer.

"A deal? he echoed, his voice hinting skepticism. "Ya tink ya can bargain wit' me?"

"Listen, I got a connect with the Colombians. I get pure fish scale, straight from the source. We're moving it through appliance stores, hiding it in detergent boxes. It's flying off the shelves. I got Georgia on lock, and I'm looking to expand. You can handle Florida, if we partner up, we will take over the South together."

Biggs tilted his head, a flicker of interest sparking in his eyes. "And why should I trust you? What makes ya tink your dope is better than mine?" He questioned.

Khi smirked despite the pain chewing at his insides. "It's not a question of thinking. I know! My product is purer than anything out there. Given the circumstances, I'm offering you something you can't get anywhere else. A hundred keys at 1.8. That's eighteen grand a key. I know you gotta be paying more than that now." Khi reasoned.

The wheels in Biggs' head turned as he weighed the offer. He was paying 2.1 for 100 keys, and while his product was decent, it was inconsistent, sometimes pure, sometimes stepped on. If Khi was telling the truth, this could be a game changer.

"And what's in it for you?" Biggs asked cautiously.

"Survival and Partnership," Khi replied without hesitation. He wasn't a coward, but he wasn't a fool either. He knew that this was the only leverage he had. "I keep Georgia, you take Florida. Together, we dominate the South. You will recoup the two mil Dame lost you in no time, and I know you'll be making more per key than you are now."

Money was power, and men like Biggs thrived on power. Killing Khi would only bring temporary pleasure, this was a chance for continuous reward.

Biggs stroked his beard quietly. He respected Khi's composure, most men in his position begged for their lives when faced with him. Dame had been one of them, groveling like a dog. But Khi? Khi had a backbone, Biggs appreciated that, and he couldn't deny the numbers made sense.

"Alright," Biggs said after a long silence. "I don't tink dis is the right time to discuss de details, we can schedule a proper meeting in a few weeks. But understand dis, if ya cross me there won't be a second chance." Biggs warned.

Khi met his gaze, his lips curling into a faint smile. "I don't believe in second chances.

Biggs chuckled darkly, his grin returning. "We'll see about dat."

▪▪▪

Chapter 4

Trinity lay sprawled across the creaky bed in the musty hotel room, staring at the water-stained ceiling as her thoughts spiraled into despair. Just weeks ago, her life had been stable, damn near perfect even. Now it had turned into chaos, each thread snapping under the weight of lies, loss, and desperation. The $7,000 she had snatched from Nicole's purse felt like a cruel joke. It wouldn't last, not when she was cut off from all Dame's accounts.

The millions Dame had left behind were useless, literally untouchable. She had no identification and was out of options. She was wanted for murder, a fugitive trapped in a life she no longer recognized. And worse, the only person she had ever truly depended on was gone, leaving her in an endless, lonely void.

"This is all that bitch Xanae's fault! I hate her!" Trinity screamed, as she grabbed fistfuls of her hair and yanked. A surge of fury coursed through her veins, and before she could stop herself, she hurled the bedside lamp across the room. It shattered against the wall, a spray of glass and frustration. She blamed Xanae for everything: losing Dame, losing Khi, losing her child. Her misplaced anger was a wildfire, consuming every rational thought.

I have nothing left to lose, she thought bitterly.

She needed to get out of the room before she lost what was left of her mind. She slipped on her shoes, grabbed the key card, and pulled the door open, desperate for fresh air. Instead of freedom, a tall, brown skinned adonis with a commanding presence stood in front of her.

Trinity froze, her heart leaping to her throat. "Can I help you?" she asked, her voice guarded as her eyes darted over him, assessing every detail.

The man flashed a quick smile. "Oh, my bad Miss Lady. I thought this was my room. I'm in 586, I guess that's why my key card wasn't working." His deep voice was smooth with a casual charm.

Trinity exhaled, her initial wariness easing. "This is 588," she replied.

"Yeah, I see that now. My mistake, but since I'm here, I might as well introduce myself. I'm Reese, and you are?"

"Trinity," she replied with a faint smile. She took a moment to really look at him. He was 6'3, with broad shoulders, mahogany skin and a perfect goatee. He was undeniably fine, and there was something about him that drew her in like a magnet. Who was this man?

She could spot a boss a mile away and it was crystal clear that Reese didn't belong in a raggedy-ass motel. It wasn't his clothes that told the story; he wasn't draped head to toe in designer labels or flashy logos. It was the way he carried himself. His stance was firm, like a man who was always in control, no matter the situation.

The deep baritone of his voice commanded attention, each word spoken with the confidence of someone used to being heard. This wasn't a man who settled. He was the kind who belonged in a five-star penthouse suite, overlooking the city skyline, his feet kicked up on an executive desk while he orchestrated moves that most people couldn't even dream of. And yet, here he was, tucked into the corner of a run-down motel, making the space feel more like his kingdom than the cheap room it actually was.

"I been here for a few months and I've never seen you before, are you visiting?" Reese asked casually as his eyes traced her body, studying her like she was a puzzle he couldn't wait to solve.

Trinity hesitated for a moment, trying to make sure she didn't say too much.

"Umm, yeah, for a little bit. I'm relocating. I've only been here about a week, just trying to figure things out," she replied.

The truth spilled from her lips before she even realized it. Her real name, her situation, she had given it all away without thinking. She immediately regretted it, but it was too late to take it back now.

"Well, I'm around for a while," Reese said, his eyes dipping briefly to her thick, smooth Butterscotch colored thighs. He didn't try to hide the way he looked at her, but his glare wasn't lewd, it was just enough to make her feel seen.

"When you need some company, I'm right next door." Reese said smoothly.

Trinity caught the subtlety in his words, he said ***when***, not ***if***. It wasn't just a casual offer; it was a certainty, as if he already knew they would be seeing each other again.

She nodded, trying to suppress a smile. Although she was more than intrigued by him, she wasn't about to let it show.

"I'll keep that in mind," she replied, her tone deliberately dry.

As she brushed past him the scent of his cologne tickled her nose, and her pulse quickened. She felt him staring at her, trailing her every step as she made her way to Nicole's car.

Sliding into the driver's seat, she let out a quiet breath she hadn't realized she was holding. He's trouble, she thought as she stuck the key in the ignition. But even as she started the car, she couldn't stop herself from grinning. It was the first time she had smiled in weeks and trouble didn't feel like something she wanted to avoid.

Trinity had been driving aimlessly through the city streets for hours, trying her hardest to figure out her next move. The reality of her situation ate away at her heavily. She wished she had someone to call, a lifeline to grasp. She knew it was just a matter of time before she hit rock bottom.

Her mind wandered back to Reese, and a slow realization dawned on her. He had been at her door for a reason, even if he didn't know it yet. She needed him, and judging by the way he had looked at her like she was something he couldn't wait to unwrap, he wanted her. The thought planted a seed that caused her to immediately head back to the hotel.

When she returned, she went straight to her room, tossing the keys onto the nightstand before stepping into the tiny bathroom. She turned on the shower, letting the water run hot as she stripped away the day's frustration.

The scent of strawberries and cream filled the steamy air as she lathered her skin, taking her time as if she could wash away the residue of her desperation. She worked conditioner into her hair, coaxing it into soft, glossy curls, then let the hot water cascade over her body until it ran cold.

After her shower she slipped into a thin tank top without a bra and a pair of shorts that hugged her hips. She had cut her hair short, in an effort to change her appearance and still needed time to adjust to the change. She quickly ran a swipe of mascara over her lashes and smoothed gloss onto her lips, the bare minimum to feel like herself. Everything she wore down to the drugstore makeup had come from Walmart, a far cry from the designer labels that once defined her wardrobe. The thought stung, but she shoved it aside. *Work with what you've got.* She thought as she ruffled her short curls with her fingers.

She caught her reflection in the mirror. For all the corners she had cut, she still had it. Her curves were fuller in all the right places after pregnancy and her skin was perfect. She took a deep breath before grabbing her key card and making her way next door to room 586.

Trinity paused at the door, hesitating just long enough for nerves to creep in. She knocked lightly, her knuckles barely touching the wood before the door swung open. Reese stood there, finer than he had been earlier. His expression remained neutral, but his eyes lit up as soon as he saw her.

"What's up beautiful," he said, stepping aside to let her in.

She smiled, the flirtation slipping naturally into her voice. "I thought I'd take you up on your offer. I'm going stir-crazy in that room all by myself, so I figured we could keep each other company." Trinity cooed. She didn't understand why Reese had her feeling like a little girl. Just being around him caused her tummy to fill with butterflies.

Reese's grin widened. "I'm glad you came, I won't lie, I been waiting. Have a seat. You want a drink?" He asked.

"Sure," Trinity replied, her eyes darting around the room as she perched on the edge of the bed. Prada sneakers lay discarded in the corner, next to a thick diamond necklace that caught the light just right.

On the nightstand sat a small stack of cash and a cluster of photographs. Trinity tried to steal a glimpse of the photos, but Reese quickly grabbed them and stuffed them in the drawer when he noticed her wandering eyes.

"You like Hennessy?" He asked, interrupting her thoughts as he handed her a paper cup.

"It will do," she replied, taking a sip of the warm liquor. It burned its way down her throat, a welcome distraction from the thoughts that consumed her.

Reese poured himself a drink and settled into the chair across from her. "So, where you from?" He asked.

"Texas," Trinity lied quickly, taking another sip of her drink before looking up at him. "What about you?"

"I'm from everywhere," Reese replied with a shrug. "I don't stay in one place too long. I'm just here right now to handle some things with my family."

"I don't have any family," Trinity said, her voice softening. "I'm here by myself, I still haven't decided where I'm going to end up." She said truthfully.

"You don't think you're gonna like Maryland huh?" Reese asked, his eyes fixed on her as he refilled her cup.

"I don't know yet," Trinity replied, finishing her drink in one gulp, before holding out the cup for more. She felt her guard slipping with each sip, the alcohol spreading through her limbs loosening the tight knot of tension that caused her gut to ache in nervousness. He was slowly breaking her defenses.

The next morning, Trinity woke to the sunlight filtering through the thin hotel curtains. She stretched as she inhaled the faint scent of Reese's cologne clinging to the sheets.

Memories of the night before came flooding back. She recalled his easy laughter, the way he looked at her like she was the most interesting thing in the room, the haze of smoke and alcohol that had lulled her into comfort. It had been years since she'd felt that kind of ease with a man.

She sat up, her eyes scanning the room for him. She heard the bathroom door open and turned her head just in time to see him step out, with his grey sweatpants hanging low on his hips. Her eyes traced the outline of his manhood, bold and unfiltered against the thin fabric.

"Good morning," Reese said, his voice deep and smooth as he sat on the edge of the bed.

Trinity smirked, pulling the covers up lazily around her. "Good morning. I see I woke up in your bed. You didn't try to steal any of my goodies, did you?" She playfully asked.

Reese chuckled as he looked into her eyes. "Nah, Miss Lady. I don't want anything I have to take. I like to earn mine." He replied.

“Who is this Man?” Trinity thought as she looked at him with lustful eyes. Reese knew all the right things to say, his words wrapped around her like a slow-burning flame. It had been so long since she had felt this way, so long since a man had looked at her like she was something special. She had wasted years on Dame’s cheating, manipulative ass, chasing scraps of his attention. Somewhere along the way she had forgotten what it felt like to be seen, to be desired by a man who seemed to mean every word he said.

Damn, this man might actually be the truth. She thought as

she slid off the edge of the bed then straightened her shorts, letting her fingers linger for just a moment. "I guess I should get back to my room. I had fun last night. Maybe we can do it again before you leave town." She said, pretending that she wasn’t pressed to spend more time with him.

Reese leaned back in the chair and smirked.

"Me too, but don't go just yet, I ordered breakfast. Ima go pick it up, and when I get back there's something I wanna talk to you about."

Trinity's brow lifted slightly, curiosity prickling at the edges of her thoughts.

"Something like what?" she asked, her voice steadier than she felt. Butterflies fluttered in her stomach, a warning, and a thrill colliding inside her. For the first time, the thought crossed her mind that Reese knew more about her than he let on.

"You'll find out, just stay here." He said, as he stood, and quickly headed out, leaving her rooted in place as the door clicked shut behind him.

As soon as he was gone Trinity's eyes wandered. The stack of crisp hundred-dollar bills on the dresser caught her attention first, the edges of the notes peeking out like a silent invitation. Right next to it sat the diamond necklace that sparkled against the hotel lights, mocking her restraint. *It's right there. No one would know,* she thought, her hand twitching toward the haul. But something deep inside held her back, a voice whispering that taking it would cost more than she was willing to pay. Instead, she slipped into the bathroom, splashed cold water on her face and stared at her reflection. "What are you doing, Trinity?" she asked herself, shaking her head. She didn't have an answer, at least not one she wanted to admit.

When Reese returned, the room filled with the smell of fresh coffee and syrup. He sat the bags down on the bed and started unpacking them, the rhythm of his movements drawing her in even more.

"I didn't know what you liked, so I ordered a little bit of everything" he said, flashing her that same disarming smile.

Trinity reached for a bowl of fruit, grabbed a strawberry, and popped it into her mouth. The sweet tang burst on her tongue, momentarily grounding her.

"This is nice of you, but what did you want to talk about?"

Reese glanced at her, his dark eyes glinting with something she couldn't quite place.

"Don't take this the wrong way, but the first time I saw you something in your eyes told me that you can handle any situation that's thrown your way. I don't know what you running from but eventually you have to stop running."

The strawberry nearly lodged in Trinity's throat, she coughed, her voice rising in unease.

"What? What makes you think that?" She asked. *Did he recognize her, did he somehow know about the grim details of her past?*

Reese chuckled, his laugh low and unapologetic. "Like I said, it's in your eyes," he repeated. "I can tell that you're just like me, and that's not a bad thing. I need somebody like you."

Trinity's confusion deepened, her thoughts spinning. "What do you mean, somebody like me?" she asked defensively.

"Someone fine, someone observant, someone with grit," Reese said matter-of-factly. "I have an opportunity for you to make a lot of paper, but I need to know that you can trust me, I need you to follow my lead and be willing to learn.

Trinity's heart thumped against her ribs as his words settled over her. She didn't have many options, and a steady paycheck from a nine-to-five wasn't in the cards for her.

"I'm willing to hear you out," she said finally.

Reese stood, gathering his things with a precision that suggested he had already made up his mind about her. "Let's go," he said simply.

Moments later Trinity slipped on her shoes and followed Reese outside, her curiosity outweighing her apprehension. He escorted her towards his black Denali that sat in the lot.

"Where are we going?" she asked as she hopped into the passenger seat, her fingers trailing over the leather interior.

Reese didn't even look her way as he started the engine, his focus locked on moving to his next destination.

He had wrecked his brain for weeks trying to figure out how to get his next job completed. Meeting Trinity was a means to an end.

"I got a job in D.C., The pay is good, and the effort is minimal. I got 50 bands for you when we're done." Reese explained, knowing there were few people willing to turn down such a large amount of money.

Trinity's eyes widened at the mention of $50,000. That kind of money would be life-changing for her right now. The thought of it sent a spark of excitement through her, a momentary reprieve from the reality of her current situation. But as quickly as the excitement came, it was chased by a bitter reminder that less than a year ago, fifty grand was nothing to her. Pocket change, she thought sadly. Back then, she dropped that kind of money on shoes and designer purses. Now, it felt like salvation dangled just out of reach.

Reese kept talking, laying out the job in broad strokes. He made it sound easy, routine even. But something about the way he spoke made it clear that this wasn't a request. His tone wasn't asking; it was telling. He had already decided that she was the one who would help him get it done.

Trinity stared at him as she leaned back and tried to take everything in. He was calm, but there was an edge to him, a quiet authority that demanded obedience. The way he said it, like the outcome had already been written sent a shiver down her spine while simultaneously turning her on.

She shifted in her seat, fighting the mix of unease and intrigue that bubbled inside her. "What kind of job is this?" she asked curiously.

"You'll find out soon enough" Reese said, glancing at her briefly.

“Why me? You don’t even know me. You said yourself you think I’m running from something.”

"I do,” Reese admitted. “But you proved that I can trust you. I left that paper and my jewels on purpose just to see what you would do while I was gone."

“Well, what would have happened if I had run off with everything?" Trinity asked.

Reese chuckled, his hand hovering over a button on his keychain. "Then you wouldn’t have made it far," he said, pressing the button just before he drove out of the motel parking lot.

A deafening BOOM shattered the quiet as a fiery explosion erupted behind them. Trinity’s heart raced as she whipped around, her breath catching in her throat at the sight of Nicole’s car engulfed in flames. The roar of the fire drowned out the thoughts running rampant in her mind as she stared, wide-eyed, at the burning wreckage.

She looked back to Reese, who kept his eyes on the road, his expression disturbingly calm. In that moment, Trinity's unease turned to certainty. He wasn't just trouble, he was lethal, and now she was strapped in beside him, headed into the unknown.

Chapter 5

"It's three in the morning. Where the hell is she?" Khi muttered, pacing the living room in agitated circles. He had barely set foot in the house before noticing the empty driveway. Xanae's car was gone, and the silence inside felt colder than he expected. After almost a week of agony and striking a dangerous deal with Biggs just to make it back alive, this wasn't the homecoming he had envisioned.

Biggs had kept his word, arranging transportation back to Georgia as part of their deal. Khi knew that he should've called Xanae the moment he was given a chance to, but he wanted to explain his absence face to face.

He was desperate to see his woman, to hold his son, to feel the comfort of home. Instead, he was met with darkness and emptiness. His mind raced with every worst-case scenario playing out in vivid detail. *If she missed me, she would be here, waiting, crying, hoping.* He thought. It was early morning hours, and Xanae still hadn't been home. Khi couldn't help but wonder- *Did she already know about Trinity? Had she left him for good?* When he noticed that all of her stuff was still there he tried to reassure himself that this was not the end. Without a phone, he couldn't call her a million times or check to see if his messages were delivered. He decided to wait, wait and let his emotions simmer.

Hours went by and Khi hadn't slept a single second. As the waiting game continued, the clock's ticking scraped at his nerves like nails on a chalk board. Resting was impossible, unthinkable until he set eyes on Xanae. Not until he could inhale her scent, that intoxicating mix of vanilla and the natural pheromones of her skin that stuck with him like a memory he didn't deserve to keep. He needed to feel her warmth, the press of her body against his, to reassure himself that she still loved him, still trusted him, still saw a future with him despite everything they had been through. But the weight of what he hadn't told her clawed at him, heavy and insistent. He hadn't spoken to anyone since Biggs had taken him and couldn't be sure how much Xanae knew about the details surrounding his disappearance.

He knew that she was safe and that there was no need to run through the city like a mad man searching for her, he could feel it in the way his pulse steadied at the thought of her. But even that fragile comfort couldn't drown out the truth looming in the back of his mind. Trinity was still alive. The lie he had told Xanae to keep them together, to shield her from worry, now sat on his brain like a ticking time bomb. And when it exploded, Khi didn't know if Xanae would still be there or if this would be the thing to break them for good.

The fear of losing her caused a lump to form in his throat, making it hard to breathe. He had seen the heartbreak in her eyes before, but this? This could shatter her. It Could shatter both of them. He knew he needed to tell her the truth, but he wasn't ready to face that. Not now, not ever.

Every shadow that flickered outside the window made his heart race; every creak of the floorboards teased his hope. He kept glancing at the door, willing it to swing open and for her to step inside. The prayer was silent but desperate, a raw plea to a God he hadn't spoken to very often.

"God Please let her come back. Please let her forgive me when she finds out the truth" Khi prayed.

He sank into the couch, dragging a hand through his hair, tugging at the roots as if pain could keep him grounded. His heartbeat thudded so loud and heavy; it seemed to echo in the quiet of the room. How had he let it come to this? How had he thought he could protect her with lies when the truth was already tearing them apart?

No matter how much the shame ate at him, no matter how much the regret burned in his chest, he knew one thing for certain: Xanae was his life. His peace. His reason to keep going. Even if it took every ounce of strength he had to fix what he had broken, to earn her trust again, he would do it. He just prayed it wasn't already too late.

By the time the sun started to rise Khi was exhausted. Finally, around 9:00 AM, the sound of a car pulling into the driveway shattered the unbearable silence. He shot to his feet as Xanae walked through the door, her expression shifting the moment she saw him. Shock flashed across her face before it hardened into something he didn't expect.

"Where you been Nae?" Khi asked, his voice brimming with barely restrained anger. He crossed the room in two quick strides, his frustration boiling over.

Xanae froze for a split second, her eyes wide as if she had just seen a ghost. Then her shoulders squared, and the surprise on her face was replaced with defiance. She remembered what Rock had told her, that Khi needed space, that he had left to clear his head. How dare he stand here now, demanding answers after disappearing for days!

"Khi? Are you serious right now? "I've been at Rock and Shiyah's. They're watching KJ. What are you doing here?" Xanae replied crossing her arms defensively.

Khi blinked and slightly cocked his head, caught off guard by her tone. "What do you mean what am I doing here Ma? I live here, right?" He questioned.

"I don't know! Do you?!," Xanae shot back, her voice rising. "I haven't seen you in days, and now you just pop up out of nowhere like nothing happened. Nah. You should've stayed wherever the fuck you were at!" She yelled angrily as she turned on her heels to walk past him.

"Yo, chill with all that!" Khi snapped, as he stepped in her path and grabbed her arm. His grip was firm but not rough, his frustration turning into desperation. “You don’t know what I been through these last few days Nae. Sit down so we can talk.” He demanded.

Xanae jerked her arm out of his grasp, her eyes blazing. “Talk? You wanna talk now Khi?” She laughed sarcastically. “Where was all this energy when you ghosted us? You left me alone with KJ after everything I just went through, and now you wanna act like I owe you a conversation?”

“I didn’t ghost you Nae,” Khi shot back, his voice rising to match hers. “You don’t know where I been or why I was gone! The whole time I was fighting to come home, and now that I’m here, you giving me this shit?” Khi questioned.

“Don’t turn this around on me,” Xanae snapped, stepping closer until they were nearly face-to-face. Her finger jabbed into his chest, her voice mixed with fury and hurt. “You left me to pick up the pieces Khi. I needed you, and you weren't here! Do you know what that felt like? To think that you might be dead, or worse?" Xanae cried.

Khi bit the inside of his cheek, her words cut deep. He had spent days fighting for his life, desperate to make it back to her and KJ, but now he realized how much his absence had cost her. Her anger was a shield, protecting wounds she tried so hard to hide.

"Nae..." His voice softened, but she cut him off with a sharp shake of her head.

"Don't 'Nae' me! You don't get to come back like this and act like everything is fine. You left me hanging Khi. You don't know what that did to me."

Khi swallowed hard before responding. "You're right," he admitted finally, his tone low but sincere. "I wasn't here when I should have been. But I'm here now. Let me fix this."

For a moment neither of them spoke, the air between them was heavy. Khi stared at her as he stepped closer.

“I love you Xanae, just let me explain, let me make this right.” he said quietly, praying she would hear him out.

Her eyes searched his, the anger in them flickering like a candle caught in the wind. She wanted to believe him; to let herself feel the relief she had craved for days. But trust didn’t come easily, not after everything that had happened.

"You called Rock, but you couldn’t call me?” Xanae cried. “I’ve been worried sick about you Khi. You left me and our son here so you could 'clear your head'?” What kind of weak ass shit is that?!”

Her words came out in a rush, anger and hurt brewing together, each one angrier than the last.

"Clear my head? What you talking about Nae?" "I been in Florida. Some Jamaican niggas snatched me out my truck and had me tied up over that dope I got from Dame. If I could've called you, I would have, and you know that!

"Do I know that Khi?! Rock told me he talked to you!" Xanae screamed, her glare cutting through him like ice.

"He told you what?" Khi's brows furrowed, confusion flashing across his face. "I haven't talked to Rock since right before it happened. We were supposed to meet up to tie up some loose ends, but shit took a turn. I didn't tell you because I wanted it to be a surprise, but I bought us a new crib. I went over there to check on some shit, and a nigga caught me from behind and knocked me out. Next thing I know, I'm tied to a chair in some dark-ass room." Khi replied.

Xanae shook her head, her laugh was cold. "You expect me to believe that? It sounds a lot like the same story I told you when I was taken from the hospital. Is this your way of trying to get back at me?" She asked.

Her words hit Khi like a slap, he stared at her, disbelief etched across his face. "You ain't gotta believe me, but it's the truth Nae. Where is this shit coming from? Since when don't you trust me?" He asked.

Xanae's lip quivered. "I don't know Khi. It's like crazy shit keeps happening to us back-to-back, and I don't know what to believe anymore. I'm just tired. I can't take anymore of this."

Her strength crumbled as the tears she'd been holding back spilled down her cheeks. She felt her knees getting weak, and Khi caught her before she could fall, pulling her into his arms. She clung to him, her sobs muffled against his chest, her anger melting into vulnerability.

Khi held her tightly, his hand running soothingly over her back as he whispered, “I’m here now Nae. I got you Baby. Whatever’s coming at us, we’ll handle it together. You hear me?”

Xanae nodded against his chest, his embrace momentarily quieting the storm inside her. She wanted to believe him, to trust that the man holding her could protect her from whatever trouble or cruelty the world had to offer, but in the back of her mind the shadows of doubt persisted, whispering that the worst might still be yet to come.

“Baby, you are my life, I would never lie to you about something like this. Everything I’m doing is for us. I’m sorry for what I put you through, but I need you to trust me Nae.” Khi pleaded.

He held her close, stroking her hair as if trying to smooth away the turmoil between them. He lifted her gently and carried her to the couch, his arms cradling her like she was the most precious thing in the world. As he sat her down, his lips found the soft curve of her neck.

His hands moved to the hem of her dress, lifting it slowly over her head. The tension in the room shifted and was replaced with an intimate urge that they both craved. It had been 6 long weeks since Xanae had given birth to KJ, and every inch of Khi's body burned with the need to reconnect with her. He unclasped the black lace bra she wore with a practiced touch, letting it fall away. Her panties didn't stand a chance, he ripped them off in one swift motion, his hunger for her undeniable.

Xanae gasped as Khi trailed his tongue across her stomach, her voice thick with pleasure as his lips found the sensitive skin of her inner thighs.

Her fingers tangled in his dreads, pulling gently as his tongue parted her folds, finding her clit with precision. Khi's moans vibrated against her pearl, his satisfaction evident as he worshiped her body. The moment felt deeper, heightened by the distance they had endured and the chaos that had threatened to pull them apart.

His hands moved to her breasts, kneading them gently as his tongue slowly circled her sweet spot. Xanae's back arched, her screams filling the room as waves of pleasure rolled over her, causing her body to tremble under his touch. Khi groaned in satisfaction, savoring the taste of her juices as they flowed into his mouth.

"I love you Nae," Khi said as he lifted her leg over his shoulder. His eyes locked with hers as he waited for her permission, her confirmation that her body could handle it and that she wanted him to keep going.

"I love you too baby, I love you so much Khi" Xanae moaned as she squirmed in anticipation.

"I love you more than life Ma." Khi whispered just as she placed both hands on his upper back and pulled him closer.

He pushed into her slowly, her warmth enveloping him, and they both gasped at the connection. Khi's lips found her calf, he slowly kissed her leg and nibbled on her ankle softly as her walls gripped him, pulling him deeper. Each thrust was intentional, a deliberate rhythm that spoke volumes about his love and need for her. It was more than just physical, it was a reminder of their bond, a promise in every movement.

Xanae's nails dug into his shoulders as their passion intensified, their bodies moving as one until the pressure became too much and they both exploded. Khi groaned her name loudly, his release a powerful culmination of his love, pain, and longing.

As her breathing slowed, Xanae nestled into his arms, her body limp with satisfaction and exhaustion. Sleep claimed her quickly, her soft breaths a quiet melody against his chest.

Khi's mind refused to rest. He gritted his teeth as her earlier words replayed in his head. *Rock said he talked to me?* The claim fed a suspicion he had ignored for far too long. He noticed the way Rock watched Xanae, the subtle questions he asked about her, the way his face lit up when she entered the room. Khi had brushed it off, dismissing it as paranoia, but now it was clear that Rock wasn't just a friend looking out for his woman. He wanted Xanae to be his.

Khi's grip on Xanae tightened protectively as his thoughts darkened. Rock had crossed a line, and whatever vendetta he had, Khi was about to end it. One way or another, he was going to set this shit straight.

Ahhhh! Oh my God Khi, I love it!" Xanae shrieked, her hands covered her mouth as her eyes widened in awe. She stood frozen for a moment, staring up at the massive mansion that was now hers. The house was a vision of perfection, everything she had ever dreamed of and more. As soon as the car came to a stop, she practically jumped out, unable to contain her excitement. She stood by the front door, bouncing on her toes as she waited for Khi.

The mansion stood tall and proud, its 6,000 square feet of elegance framed by lush, manicured lawns and a driveway that seemed to stretch forever. Khi held KJ snugly in his arms as he unlocked the door with a slight smirk. Xanae let out another gasp as the door swung open, revealing the splendor inside.

The interior was breathtaking. Cream and gold accents adorned every room, giving the home a timeless, regal feel. The grand foyer featured a sweeping staircase with intricate wrought-iron railings, and a massive chandelier that hung like a crown, casting a soft, golden glow across the marble floors. Every corner of the space spoke of class, and Xanae felt as if she had stepped into a dream.

Her excitement increased as she moved from room to room taking it all in. The seven bedrooms were sprawling retreats, each with its own unique charm, and the nine bathrooms sparkled with lavish fixtures and imported tile.

“Oh my God Khi!” Xanae exclaimed, her voice echoing through the vast space. “This is more beautiful than I could’ve ever imagined.”

Khi leaned against the wall with a satisfied smile on his face as he watched her. Seeing her happy made all the risks, the late nights, and the dangerous deals worth it. This moment was his reward.

“I’m glad you like it Ma,” he said, stepping closer and sliding his free arm around her waist. “I chose it because I felt like it was perfect, just like you.” His lips met hers in a tender kiss, and Xanae melted into him, her joy radiating in every touch.

“When can we move in?” she asked eagerly.

“Today if you want, but we don’t have much furniture yet.” Khi said with a chuckle.

"Oh don't worry about that, we will have everything we need by the end of the day." Xanae replied with a mischievous grin.

Khi raised an eyebrow, knowing this was going to be an all-day affair.

"Alright," he said reluctantly. "But I don't want you going by yourself. I gotta meet up with Rock to discuss some business. After that, I'll take you wherever you wanna go."

Xanae nodded, her smile never wavering. She was already mentally arranging furniture in each room, planning the color schemes and personal touches she would add to make this house their home.

But Khi's thoughts were elsewhere. The new spot was opening in four days, and the meeting with Rock was supposed to be about inventory and last-minute updates.

He tried hard to come up with a valid reason for why Rock lied, but there wasn't one. Khi's heart rate increased as he thought about it. It felt like a challenge; one he couldn't let slide. Business was one thing, but no one disrespected his family.

He looked back at Xanae, who was now gushing over the walk-in closet in the master bedroom. He would give her the world and go to war with anyone who tried to take it, or her away from him.

Money had to be made so he had to continue handling business as usual, but he was still going to have a long-overdue conversation with Rock.

Rock pulled into the warehouse lot, a sinking feeling settled in his gut when he spotted Khi's truck parked near the entrance. Khi's call yesterday had been like a punch to the chest, unexpected and impossible to ignore.

When Khi went missing Rock didn't make a single move to find him. Instead, he told Xanae and the crew that Khi was fine, just laying low to clear his head. It was an easy lie, one that no one other than Xanae had questioned.

But now? Khi was back, and Rock knew this meeting wasn't going to be business as usual. As much as he hated to admit it, Xanae wasn't the only reason he had been hoping Khi would stay out of the picture. Deep down, Rock was salty about how quickly Khi had come in and taken over. For years the crew had been his. He had built them from the ground up, brick by brick he turned nobodies into soldiers who ran the streets like well-oiled machines. When Khi first arrived, Rock thought that they would be partners, but instead Khi had taken the reins, and now Rock felt like he was working for him. He had been the one to introduce

Khi to Cruz, the one who laid the foundation for everything they were doing now. Yet he was stuck playing second in command while Khi reaped the rewards, money, respect and power. It didn't sit right with him, it never had.

Rock took a deep breath as he stepped inside the warehouse. Khi was already seated at the center table. The faint hum of fluorescent lights filled the silence, making the tension in the air even more pronounced.

"My nigga! Boy, I'm glad you aite!" Rock said, forcing a grin and extending his hand as he approached the table.

Khi didn't move. His face was stone-cold; his eyes locked onto Rock with a loud intensity.

"Yeah, I bet," Khi said flatly. He motioned to the chair across from him. "Sit down. We need to talk."

Rock hesitated but quickly masked his nerves, sliding into the chair as if everything was cool. "What's up?" he asked casually.

Khi leaned back in his chair, his eyes analyzed Rocks every move. "How much was in the shipment?"

"Fifty bricks, just like we ordered. Another fifty's coming next week," Rock replied, his voice was even, but his hands fidgeted on the table.

"Good. Now that we've got the business handled, let's talk about something else" Khi said, his tone changing.

Rock shifted in his seat, feigning ignorance. "What's up fam? Everything good?"

Khi's eyes narrowed into slits. "I don't know. You tell me. You eating good right?"

"Hell yeah, It's gravy over here. Just ready to get the spot up and running so we can bring in more paper." Rock replied quickly, though his nerves were starting to show.

Khi smirked, but there was no humor in it. "So, if everything is good, if you eating and your plate stays full, then this ill feeling I'm getting from you ain't about money. Let me ask you something Rock. When you showed up at my crib that day and saw that I wasn't there, what did you tell Xanae and the crew?"

Rock froze for a split second before slipping on a practiced mask of confusion. "Ill feeling? I don't know what you getting at fam. All I told them was that I had just talked to you and that you probably needed to get away to clear your head. I ain't want nobody getting all worked up over nothing. I knew you were good" he lied, trying to stay calm but his body was tense.

Khi's eyes bore into Rock like he could see straight through him. "You couldn't have known that because I wasn't good. I got caught up with some Jamaicans down in Florida. They snatched me out my truck, had me tied up and shit for days. Now we're locked into business with them. It's time to expand the operation, in a few months they will be moving our product in Florida, same strategy, different soldiers. This shit was definitely unexpected, but it will benefit us in the long run." Khi explained.

Rock leaned back, swallowing hard. "Shit, word? Damn man, I didn't know. If I did, you know we would've had an army out there looking for you. I'm just glad you back bruh." He said, his voice dripping with faux concern.

Khi leaned forward, his hands clasped together on the table. "Yeah, that's good to hear Rock, because I'm gonna say this once and only once. Don't give me a reason to question your loyalty. I don't trust too many people, and if I find out you crossing me, whether it's with my business or my woman this shit ain't gone end good."

"Your woman?" Rock scoffed, leaning back in his chair with a forced chuckle. "Come on man. Xanae is like a sister to me. I don't know what she told you, but I was just trying to look out for her and KJ. That's all. It seems like she's been tripping ever since all that shit happened with Trinity."

Khi's expression didn't shift. He studied Rock, dissecting every word that came out of his mouth. He could feel the lies in every nervous fidget. He knew Rock was full of shit, but for now, he let it slide. "Let him think he's playing Chess. Let him feel like he's ahead". Khi thought. Khi wasn't the type to make a move without knowing exactly where all the pieces were on the board. One thing was clear, if Rock was dumb enough to cross him, then he needed to be ready to face the consequences. Rock could spin the story with excuses and act like he was just looking out, but Khi's instincts told him there was more to it. And his instincts were rarely wrong.

"I hope that's true for your sake," Khi said menacingly.

The room fell silent, Rock shifted uncomfortably but kept his face neutral, trying to ignore the bead of sweat that prickled at the back of his neck.

Khi finally transitioned back to business. "We're leaving for Florida in a few weeks. Get the crew in line and make sure they're ready to hold shit down while we gone. Call Blaze and Noriega, make sure they have everything set for the Grand Opening." Khi instructed.

Rock nodded, eager to move past the tension. "I got you" he said quickly, pulling out his phone to take notes.

As the conversation turned back to inventory and logistics, Rock's mind was stuck on Khi's warning. He thought he could play this game, but now he wasn't so sure. Khi wasn't the kind of man you crossed lightly, and Rock was running out of moves.

As if he were reading his mind, Khi stood, adjusting his jacket as he prepared to leave. "Don't let me find out you moving funny Rock. You don't wanna test me on this."

Without waiting for a response, Khi walked out of the warehouse, leaving Rock alone at the table.

Chapter 6

Trinity felt like she was floating. She had only known Reese for a couple of weeks, but being with him felt so natural, like they had known each other forever. He gave her something she hadn't experienced in years: attention, care, and affection. After a lifetime of feeling like an afterthought, she finally felt seen. For the first time, Trinity allowed herself to believe that someone truly cared about her.

Reese trailed his fingers lazily across her skin, his touch warm and featherlight as he traced the scars on her stomach.

"You never told me how you got these," he said curiously.

Trinity froze, her heartbeat increasing, her mind racing. She had hoped he wouldn't ask about her past. Honesty wasn't something she could afford to share, not with the life she had lived. She shifted slightly, her face calm, masking the lie she was about to spin.

"I haven't been completely honest with you," she began, her voice trembling just enough to sound convincing. "The truth is, I was in an abusive relationship. When I tried to leave, he shot me. I woke up in the hospital a couple of months ago lucky to be alive. I knew I had to get away, so I left with nothing but a few thousand dollars and the clothes on my back."

The lie rolled off her tongue effortlessly, her talent for deception as sharp as ever. She liked Reese more than she had expected, but she knew she couldn't be honest with him. Her past was a labyrinth of secrets, and if Reese ever found out the truth, he would surely run. Or worse. So she did what she always did, she lied.

Reese's expression softened as he pulled her closer. "Damn Ma. I'm sorry that happened to you, but you don't ever have to worry about that nigga as long as you're with me. I got you."

His voice was filled with a tenderness that made Trinity's heart full. Before she could respond, Reese gently flipped her over and began to lick the back of her neck. His kisses were slow, and passionate, igniting a fire beneath her skin. Trinity closed her eyes as she enjoyed the sensation of his hands on her skin.

Initially, Reese saw Trinity as a means to an end, someone to help him with the job he had coming up. But after spending time with her something changed. She wasn't just a tool; she was becoming someone he wanted. Someone he cared about.

Trinity shivered as Reese's hands moved down her body, sliding her panties off with one hand. She moaned softly, her body arching into his touch as he parted her legs, his fingers moving in slow, teasing circles.

"Reeese, babbbbyy," she whined, her voice heavy with need. "That feels so good. Please don't stop."

Reese didn't respond. He let his actions speak for him, leaning down to replace his fingers with his mouth. His hot tongue flicked against her clit, sending her into euphoria. Trinity's moans filled the room, raw and uninhibited as he worked her body like he had memorized every inch of her. He held her hips firmly, his tongue moving with a rhythm that pushed her closer and closer to the edge. When her body began to tremble and her juices overflowed, he lapped up every drop, savoring the taste of her honey.

Trinity was still trying to catch her breath when she felt Reese move behind her. He positioned himself carefully, his body weight pressing against her as he slowly slid his thickness into her pussy. A gasp escaped her lips, followed by a cry of pleasure as he filled her completely. Her back arched instinctively, her fingers clutching the sheets as he began to move, each stroke feeling like it touched her soul.

"Ahhh, oh my God, Reese please," she cried out, her voice trembling with ecstasy. "What are you doing to me?"

Reese leaned forward, his lips brushing against her ear. "Tell me you're mine," he whispered.

Trinity's moans grew louder, but she didn't answer. She couldn't. Words felt impossible in the haze of satisfaction consuming her. Instead, she let her body respond, meeting his every thrust with a hunger that matched his own.

Reese gripped her hips tighter, his strokes growing deeper, harder, more demanding. He didn't need her words, her moans told him everything he needed to know. In that moment, she was his, and he wasn't going to let her forget it.

"I said, tell me you're mine. Tell me this is my pussy," Reese commanded as his thrusts quickened, pushing Trinity closer to the edge.

"It's yours! It's your pussy!" Trinity screamed as waves of pleasure consumed her. Her walls tightened around him, and her body shook uncontrollably as the heat between them reached its peak.

Reese felt her climax building and began moving faster, his strokes becoming even more intentional. His own release crashed over him in sync with hers, and they both cried out, their bodies locked together in a moment of pure ecstasy.

They collapsed onto the bed, their breaths ragged, the air around them heavy with the scent of sex and satisfaction.

"Since we said we would be honest with each other I guess I might as well tell you what type of work I do." Reese said after a long silence. He knew that this was the perfect moment to tell Trinity what he needed her to do. Her mind and her body were weak! She was right where he wanted her.

Trinity propped herself up on one elbow to look at him. "Okay, I'm listening," she replied curiously. Truthfully, she didn't care if he sold oranges by the freeway or worked a nine-to-five. After what he had just done to her body, she wasn't planning on going anywhere.

Reese turned his head to meet her gaze, his expression serious. "I get paid to kill people," he said bluntly.

Trinity blinked, caught off guard by the casual way he said it. "What? Ha ha, very funny. What do you really do?" she asked, laughing nervously as she studied his face for any sign of a joke.

"This ain't no joke Ma," Reese replied, his voice calm and even. "I handle shit for people, people who don't wanna get their hands dirty, or who can't get close enough to take care of their targets themselves. It's not for everybody, and if it ain't for you, I get it. But if you're planning on sticking around, I need to know I can trust you.

You don't just walk away from this whenever you feel like it. You gotta be down to ride."

Trinity fell back against the pillows, her mind racing as she replayed his words. For a moment, she went back and forth with her thoughts, weighing the gravity of what he had just revealed. She wasn't in a position to judge anyone, not after everything she had done. The number of people she had killed was too high to count, and she had crossed every moral line known to man a long time ago.

"When is our first job?" she asked finally, with a small smile, as she leaned in to kiss him. Her response was confident, without hesitation.

Reese's brows lifted slightly, as if he were surprised by her response. "That's what I like to hear," he said, pulling her closer.

As she settled back against his chest, Trinity's thoughts turned darker. Meeting Reese felt like fate, like the universe had finally handed her an ally who shared her ability to kill without remorse. She hadn't told him everything yet, but knowing what Reese was capable of made one thing clear: he would be instrumental in her plan to eliminate that bitch Xanae once and for all.

A month had flown by, and now Khi and Rock found themselves in Florida, preparing to meet with Biggs. As their car rolled through the large-iron gates of Bailey Manor, Khi's eyes widened at the sheer scale of the estate. The sprawling property dwarfed the massive home he had recently purchased, its manicured lawns and towering palm trees framing the mansion like a scene straight out of a movie.

"Damn, this nigga must be moving crazy bricks." Rock muttered, his eyes sweeping over the vast property.

A guard escorted them through the marble-lined hallways of the mansion, past large chandeliers and artwork that probably cost more than most people made in a lifetime. They were led to a large suite, where Biggs lounged on a flawless white leather sectional, a thick blunt resting between his fingers. The room was filled with the scent of premium weed and the faint thump of reggae music playing in the background.

"Khi, whaa gwan," Biggs greeted with a wide grin, motioning for them to join him.

"What's good man," Khi replied, his tone light but professional as he gestured to Rock. "This is my right-hand, Rock."

Rock extended his hand, shaking Biggs' with a firm grip before they all settled into the plush seating. Khi and Rock both knew this wasn't just a casual meeting; it was a critical step toward expanding their empire.

Biggs leaned back, exhaling a cloud of smoke as he got straight to the point. "I talked to my connect out of Jamaica. He is not pleased that I'm considering severing ties. Dis gwan cost me a lot of money to end de relationship, I need to be sure dat doing business with you is de best option in de long run." He explained, his voice heavy with his island accent.

Biggs passed the blunt to Khi, who took a deep pull. The smoke hit harder than anything he had ever had before, he had to brace himself, leaning back slightly as he let it fill his lungs. He nodded in approval, exhaling slowly before passing it to Rock.

"That's ganja straight from de islands, It naw get better than det." Biggs said with a laugh.

"No doubt," Khi said with a grin, his voice steady as he shifted gears to business. "I'ma need about a pound of that before I go. Let's get to the numbers tho, how many bricks will you need per month to satisfy your clientele?"

"At least 200 per month," Biggs replied. "You tink ya connect can handle det?"

"Whatever you need, we got," Khi said confidently. "If you moving 200 a month, I can get it to you for 3.5 mil flat. But there's one condition, he will only agree to the deal if you run things the way we do back home."

Biggs arched his eyebrow, leaning forward slightly. "And how exactly do you do tings back home?" He asked.

"I told you that we run everything through a chain of appliance stores. The product comes in on delivery trucks owned by my connect. It's disguised as laundry detergent and appears completely legit on the surface. We keep regular merchandise on the showroom floor and the product locked up in the back of the warehouse. All you gotta do is direct your clients to the stores and pick up your money. No more heat on you. The FEDS won't have a clue."

Biggs stroked his chin, nodding slowly as he processed what Khi was saying. They had discussed the basics, but the explicit details had been reserved until today. The idea was genius! Cocaine disguised as laundry detergent meant less risk, less exposure. He once believed that his territory was the safest place to conduct big business. In his fortress he knew that there were no lurking shadows, no hidden wires, no watchful eyes. Every inch of it was controlled by him, secured on his terms. The idea of one of his business partners bringing malice into his sanctuary had never crossed his mind, he was a man who didn't fear much. His confidence was a wall few dared to challenge.

But lately, unease had crept in like an unwelcome guest. The visit from that nosy detective at West's funeral had rattled something in him, a quiet voice whispering that he was no longer untouchable. The more he thought about it, the more he realized that his home, once a haven, was becoming a liability. Deals like this brought risks, and even a king's castle wasn't impenetrable.

This setup Khi proposed was something else entirely. The idea of running everything through a legitimate front, clean on the surface while hiding the real operation in plain sight, was brilliant. It promised discretion, less heat, and more control. And the savings? Just on the coke alone, Biggs would be pocketing over a million dollars more each month. It was hard to ignore numbers like that.

Biggs exhaled a slow cloud of smoke, his grin widening. “When can we get de ball rolling?” he asked, his tone carrying a genuine interest that hadn’t been there before.

Khi didn’t miss a beat. “We will need a couple of weeks to secure a spot and schedule the first shipment,” he replied smoothly. His voice was calm, but inside, his excitement burned like a live wire. With Biggs on his side, Florida was practically his for the taking, and Florida was just the beginning. This deal wasn’t just about territory, it was the cornerstone of his plan for domination, a foundation he had just expertly laid.

Chapter 7

The morning sunlight filtered softly through the openings of the thick curtains of the guest bedroom, casting muted shadows across the sleek furniture and the California King bed where Khi stirred awake. The bed was vast, luxurious, and perfectly in tune with the Aesthetic of Biggs' home.

Initially, Khi had planned to stay at a hotel, he was more comfortable on neutral ground, but Biggs had insisted he and Rock accept his hospitality. It was an offer Khi had decided not to decline; building goodwill with Biggs was a calculated move, and every gesture of respect mattered in these negotiations.

Biggs also had his own motives for his hospitality, he wanted to keep a watchful eye on his newfound business partners.

The plush duvet slid off his torso as he stretched, his muscles were tense from dealing with so much stress over the past few weeks. The room itself was a sanctuary, over 700 square feet of understated elegance, with a color palette of creams and grays accented with hints of polished gold. The air smelled faintly of vanilla, a scent that seemed to permeate the entire house.

Shaking off the grogginess, Khi made his way into the attached bathroom. The space was just as impressive as the bedroom, decked with marble countertops, a rain shower head, and a huge wall-length mirror. He turned on the shower, causing the hot water to quickly envelop the room with steam. As he stepped inside, the warmth melted into his skin.

He lathered his body with the rich, fragrant soap, the scent mixing with the steam as he scrubbed away the weight of travel and business. The water cascaded over his skin, leaving him feeling renewed. After rinsing off, Khi grabbed one of the plush white towels from the rack and wrapped it securely around his waist.

Just as he stepped out of the shower, he heard the unmistakable creak of a door opening on the opposite side of the bathroom. His head snapped up, and his eyes locked onto a figure in the doorway. A beautiful, cocoa-colored woman stood there, her wide eyes mirroring his surprise.

Khi's breath hitched as he took her in. Her deep skin was smooth, and her hair fell in loose curls around her shoulders. She was dressed casually, but her presence filled the room as if she belonged there, like she was a part of the very house.

"Oh my God, I'm so sorry!" she exclaimed, her voice soft and melodic but tinged with embarrassment. Her hand flew to cover her mouth as she backed out hastily, the door clicking shut behind her.

For a moment, Khi just stood there. His mind reeled as he replayed the moment. He hadn't even realized the bathroom was a Jack and Jill layout, connecting his guest room to another.

He quickly dried off and dressed, but the image of her lingered. Who is she? He wondered. He knew Biggs' master suite was on the other side of the house, so she couldn't be his wife. It suddenly hit him that she could be his daughter.

The thought tugged at him, but something about her didn't scream daughter. There was a grace to her, an energy that felt distinctly separate from Biggs' domineering presence.

Khi finished buttoning his shirt and glanced back toward the connecting door. The encounter had been brief, but it left a mark, an unshakable curiosity that simmered in his mind. Whatever her connection to Biggs was, Khi had a feeling she wasn't just passing through.

He dressed quickly, the aroma of breakfast drifting up from downstairs spurring his pace. Biggs had made it clear the night before that breakfast was served at 9:00 AM sharp. Khi's stomach growled in agreement as he made his way down the grand staircase.

The dining room was as impressive as the rest of the house, there was a long mahogany table set impeccably, fresh fruit and steaming platters of food laid out like a feast. Khi stepped inside, his eyes immediately catching the familiar chocolate beauty he had seen earlier. She sat across from Biggs and another striking woman.

"Khi, glad ya joined us my youth," Biggs said, gesturing for him to take a seat. "Dis is my wife, Yahnni, and dis is my niece, Jade."

"Nice to meet you ladies," Khi said, as he took the seat next to Jade. Her presence was magnetic, and her beautiful storm-colored eyes made it hard to look away. Her skin was so rich and smooth it looked like silk; her beauty was almost surreal.

"Where ya man der?" Biggs asked, referring to Rock.

"That nigga probably still sleeping. Don't worry about him, we can go ahead and eat," Khi replied, doing his best to keep his focus on the conversation and not Jade's captivating smile.

The meal was a lively affair, filled with laughter and conversation. Khi found himself enjoying the company more than he expected, though his attention often drifted to Jade. She had an effortless charm about her, as she shared stories of her travels and life in Florida. He wondered how someone so vibrant could seem trapped in the gilded world Biggs had built.

When breakfast ended and the plates were cleared, Khi excused himself, retreating to the guest room to make a call to Xanae. He needed to hear her voice, to ground himself.

"Hello?" Xanae answered after a few rings.

"What's up Ma? How are you and my lil man doing?" Khi asked, leaning against the edge of the bed.

"We're good, just ready for you to come home. I miss you so much," Xanae replied softly.

"I miss you too Nae. I'll be back tomorrow, just be patient till then. Kiss KJ for me," Khi said, his voice tender. They spoke for a few more minutes before ending the call.

As he sat the phone down, a soft knock on the door startled him. Khi looked up, his eyes widening slightly as Jade stepped into the room.

"You're leaving so soon?" she asked, there was a subtle challenge in her tone.

"Yeah. I just had some business to take care of with your uncle. I gotta get back to Georgia," Khi replied, his eyes dropping briefly to her long, toned legs before snapping back to her face. Her beauty was disarming, and he couldn't remember the last time a woman other than Xanae had stirred him like this.

"Well, I need you to do me a favor before you go," Jade said.

"What's that?" Khi asked, intrigued by her sudden approach.

"You look like you're around my age, and if my uncle let you stay here, then he must trust you. I just moved to this part of Florida, and I don't know anyone. I'm always stuck in this big-ass house and I'm sick of it, I just need to get some fresh air with someone I can relate to. So come on, let's go." Jade giggled, refusing to take no for an answer.

Khi smirked, slightly amused. "Ok, I guess I can spare a few hours, I need to get familiar with Florida anyway. Let me just check on my man, see if he wanna roll."

When Khi approached Rock about joining them, he waved him off, muttering about a hangover from the night before, so they left without him.

Their first stop was Dadeland Mall, where Jade turned the shopping trip into a whirlwind of activity. Store after store, she picked out bathing suits, dresses, heels, and purses with a carefree ease. Khi couldn't help but be impressed by her confidence, though he stayed quiet, letting her lead the way.

When they left the mall, the day shifted gears. Lunch was a relaxed affair at a small café tucked into the heart of the city, and afterward, they headed to the beach. The ocean stretched as far as the eye can see and the waves rolled gently against the shore as they walked along the sand. The setting sun, bathed the sky in hues of gold and pink, casting a warm glow over the water.

Jade kicked off her sandals, letting her toes sink into the cool sand. Khi followed suit, his hands tucked into his pockets as they strolled in easy silence for a moment, the sound of the waves their only companion.

"It's getting late," Khi said finally, glancing at her. "I know your uncle is probably worried about you. We should head back Ma."

If my uncle didn't think I was in good hands, I wouldn't be here," Jade replied with a small smile, her voice soft but sure. She stopped and lowered herself onto the sand, smoothing her dress over her legs as the waves lapped quietly in the distance. The breeze played with her hair, carrying the faint scent of salt and sweetness. Khi hesitated for a moment then followed suit, sinking down beside her. He leaned back on his hands, taking in the moment. He couldn't remember the last time he felt this free. In the few hours he had spent with Jade, his usual worries had washed away. He didn't think about business, the constant shadow of his enemies or the ghosts of his past. It all seemed to fade into the background. His mind was clear for once.

"So, how often are you going to be visiting Florida?" Jade said turning toward him with a hint of curiosity in her eyes.

There was a subtle hope in her voice that she couldn't quite mask. From the moment she laid eyes on him that morning, she felt a pull toward him. It wasn't just his looks, though he was undeniably handsome. She was drawn to the way he carried himself, the confidence that radiated from him effortlessly. She had spent months grieving West, feeling the ache of loneliness that settled deep in her soul. Khi was the first man who had stirred something inside her since then.

"Maybe once a month, just to check in and make sure everything's running smooth" Khi replied.

He glanced at her, noticing how her face lit up when he said once a month. "What about you? No family? Kids? A man?"

Jade shook her head slowly, as she looked toward the ocean. "No. I lost my husband last year," she said quietly, her voice broken with sadness. "Since then, I've just been taking time to get myself together. My uncle and Yahnni were kind enough to let me stay with them."

Khi watched her closely, the vulnerability in her words catching him off guard. Her sorrow was palpable, etched into her expression as she spoke of her loss. He could feel the heaviness she carried. He understood now why she had asked him to spend the day with her, she wasn't just seeking company; she was seeking a connection, a way to fill the void left behind by her pain.

"I'm sorry Ma, I know that must be hard for you. You'll be alright though. Just take it one day at a time." Khi said sincerely. Loss was something he knew all to well, for years he had lived behind a veil, pretending that his volatile childhood didn't impact the decisions he made as a man, but the truth was they had.

Jade looked at him and smiled. There was something about Khi's steady presence that comforted her, even if she barely knew him. She wasn't ready for the evening to end, but she could sense him pulling away, retreating behind the invisible wall that men like him built to protect themselves.

Khi glanced at the sky, the sun was setting. "We should probably head back before-"

Jade didn't let him finish. She leaned forward and kissed him, her lips soft and insistent against his. The world seemed to stand still in that moment, the sound of the waves fading into the background as the warmth of her mouth consumed him. For a split second, Khi kissed her back, the temptation was too strong to fully resist.

But then, reality set in. He pulled back, breaking the kiss, though the effort cost him more than he cared to admit.

"You don't want me; you just want something because you're hurting right now. Just give it time Ma, eventually your heart will heal." he said as he put space between the two of them.

Jade's smile faded and her cheeks flushed, she wanted to respond but before she had the chance, Khi stood up and held out his hand to help her up. She hesitated before slipping her fingers into his, letting him pull her to her feet.

"I can't do this, I love my girl, and she's been through too much for me to hurt her like that." Khi said.

He didn't say it, but he felt the pull toward Jade, the fire she ignited in him with her beauty and her presence. She was tempting in a way that unsettled him, but he couldn't let himself give in. Khi made a silent vow to keep his distance, knowing it would take every ounce of willpower he had to stay away.

As they walked back toward the car the air between them was filled with unspoken tension. Khi's mind raced. It wasn't just that Jade was beautiful, it was the way she carried her pain, the quiet strength beneath her sorrow, the undeniable allure of someone both broken and resilient. It took everything in him to draw the line, to remind himself of who he was and what he already had.

But as they drove back to Biggs' house, he couldn't stop himself from looking at her out of the corner of his eye, wondering how long he could fight the temptation to taste her chocolate.

Chapter 8

Trinity took one last look in the mirror, adjusting the straps of her rhinestone-covered hot pink thong and bra top. She barely recognized the woman staring back at her. The 30-inch wavy Malaysian extensions cascaded over her shoulders, giving her an exotic edge that demanded attention.

Reese had been relentless over the past three weeks, hammering it into her head that her body had to be perfect. Every crunch, squat, and strict meal had paid off. Her stomach was as flat as a board, her hips soft and curvaceous, her ass perfectly rounded. She looked like temptation personified.

But tonight wasn't about vanity, it was about the mission.

She smoothed her butter-colored skin, the rhinestones glittering under the fluorescent lights, and felt a flicker of nervous energy in her gut. The voice of the DJ boomed over the club's sound system, cutting through her thoughts.

"We got something sweet and sticky coming to the stage for y'all tonight! Something you ain't never had before! Give it up for Hoooooonnnnney!"

The crowd roared in anticipation, the thunderous cheers reverberating through the walls. Trinity's heart thudded. She grabbed a shot of Patron from the table and downed it in one swift motion, letting the burn chase away her nerves. She exhaled sharply, then sashayed out of the dressing room in her six-inch heels, her hips swaying to the beat of K Camp's "Money Baby."

The moment she stepped onto the stage, the room erupted. The flashing neon lights danced across her skin as she moved with practiced precision. She spotted Reese in the far corner of the room, his calm, watchful eyes fixed on her. His presence steadied her; he was her anchor in this storm. Knowing he was near gave her the confidence to own the stage.

Trinity scanned the crowd, her body moving fluidly to the music. She rolled her hips and bounced her ass rhythmically, commanding the attention of every man in the room. Then she saw him, it was Kahari. He was perched in the VIP section, a glass of dark liquor in his hand. His presence was unmistakable, exuding power and control. He didn't just watch her; he studied her.

Trinity's lips curved into a sultry smile as she locked eyes with him, even when her back was to the crowd. She arched her body, looking over her shoulder and licking her lips seductively, letting him know she saw him. She moved like a pro, every gesture intentional, her body a hypnotic weapon crafted for this exact moment. The money rained down in waves- ones, fives, tens, twenties, and even a few crisp hundreds. The men in the audience were mesmerized, but her focus remained on Kahari. He was the mark.

When her set ended, Trinity collected the bundles of cash scattered across the stage, making her exit with practiced grace. She slipped into the back room to freshen up, pulling on a pair of jeans and tossing back another shot of Patron. Tonight had to be perfect, but her stomach sank when she returned to the main floor and saw Kahari's seat empty.

"Fuck!" she muttered under her breath, scanning the club. Her eyes darted from face to face, searching for him in the sea of patrons. Kahari was the King of D.C., a man who controlled every block, trap house, and dealer in the city. Taking him down wasn't just a job; it was a power play orchestrated by one of his own soldiers, someone greedy enough to want the throne for themselves.

Reese had warned her that Kahari was no ordinary man. He was always on point, never letting anyone get close enough to threaten him. That's why this wasn't a one-man job. Reese needed her, someone who could disarm Kahari in ways no man could.

They had studied him for weeks, learning his every move. He had a weakness for beautiful women and the strip club on Tuesday nights. It was the one predictable chink in his armor. Little did he know, Trinity was the blade.

Just as frustration began to set in, a low, gravelly voice whispered against her ear, sending a shiver down her spine.

"You looking for me?"

Her nerves electrified as she turned to face him. Kahari towered over her, his presence commanding.

"No, but I'm glad to know you were looking for me." She replied, her voice smooth and teasing.

Kahari smirked, his confidence radiating like heat. He leaned closer, "I want you. Meet me outside in ten minutes."

Before she could respond, he turned and walked away, his stride purposeful, as if he knew she wouldn't refuse. Trinity's mind raced as she watched him go. Reese's voice echoed in her head, reminding her of the stakes. She was no fool, she knew that this moment could make or break their entire operation.

Trinity steadied herself, took a slow breath, and smiled faintly. She was ready. She had been groomed for this moment, trained to capture his attention and exploit his weakness. Kahari had just invited her into his world. Now, it was her turn to take control.

She scanned the club again, her heart pounded as she searched for Reese. The plan was simple: Lure Kahari into one of the private rooms, seduce him just enough to lower his guard, and then finish the job. By the time anyone noticed, they would be long gone, but Kahari had flipped the script, and now Reese was nowhere to be found. Panic danced in her gut as her eyes darted through the sea of faces. When she accepted that Reese was nowhere in sight, she knew she had to make a decision. This was supposed to be their payday, the one that would set them up for months and she couldn't let it slip through her fingers.

She took a deep breath and exhaled, when she stepped outside into the sticky night air and spotted a candy-apple red Camaro idling in the parking lot. Kahari hopped out as soon as he saw her, his broad frame illuminated by the streetlights. He grabbed her arm and pulled her close.

"You came here alone?" he asked suspiciously.

"Yes. Why?" Trinity replied, fighting to keep her voice steady. Inside, her nerves rattled like dice in a cup as Kahari's hands roamed her body. To the untrained eye, his touch might have looked like lust, but Trinity knew better, she knew that he was patting her down, searching for weapons and wires.

Satisfied that she wasn't armed, Kahari's grip softened. "Get in," he said curtly, gesturing toward the passenger seat.

The drive was silent, other than the rap music blasting through the speakers. Kahari didn't speak, instead he kept his focus fixed on the road.

They pulled up to a modest brick house fifteen minutes later. Trinity stared out the window of the Camaro in confusion. She had expected a sprawling mansion with a flashy car collection in the driveway. But instead, he had brought her to what looked like a trap house.

"This is your house?" she asked with disbelief.

"I own it," Kahari replied flatly, cutting the engine. He stepped out without waiting for her, his movements careful and unhurried. Trinity hesitated for a moment, then followed him inside, her stomach twisted as she crossed the threshold. The smell of stale smoke and sweat clung to the air. Her nerves screamed for her to turn back, but she steeled herself. Backing out wasn't an option.

He led her to a room in the back that was sparsely furnished with a mattress on the floor, a mini-fridge, metal folding chair and a nightstand cluttered with empty beer bottles and a loaded gun. He grabbed a Heineken from the fridge, cracked it open, and took a long swig before tossing his shirt onto the chair. The fat on his back rippled as he moved, the pistol on the nightstand never far from reach. He collapsed onto the bed with the casual arrogance of a man who believed he was untouchable.

"Dance for me," he said, as his eyes swept over her curves.

"Dance?" Trinity echoed.

"Yeah. Do that shit you were doing at the club" Kahari replied, taking another pull from his beer before sitting it on the nightstand.

"Alright, but I need some music" Trinity said, slipping off her heels and leaning back against the wall.

Kahari smirked, grabbed his gun, and left the room. Trinity's heart raced as the sound of footsteps faded. She reached into her bra, her fingers closed around the tiny vial of cyanide Reese had given her. Time was running out, she heard the stereo in the living room blaring, and by the time he returned, she had slipped the poison into his beer.

He stepped back inside, his gun now tucked into the waistband of his jeans. His eyes lingered on her body as she stood there in her bra and panties, her curves on full display.

"Come here," Trinity purred seductively. She moved toward him slowly, her hips swaying like a pendulum, her eyes never leaving his. She pressed her body against his, then nibbled on his ear before whispering, "Fuck me daddy."

He couldn't resist, moving towards her, his eyes were glazed with lust and his breath was shallow with anticipation as he fumbled with his belt. Trinity stepped back with a sly smile on her face as she watched him take another swig of his beer.

Seconds later, Kahari froze, his body jerking violently. The bottle slipped from his hand, shattering on the floor. He clutched his chest, gasping for air as his eyes widened in panic. Trinity stood motionless; her expression cold as his body convulsed on the bed. The poison worked quickly, he struggled to breathe as he fought against the inevitable. Moments later, he stopped moving.

Trinity didn't waste a second. She quickly slipped on her jeans and heels, then headed for the door. When she stepped over Kahari's lifeless body, she felt no remorse. This was just business.

Outside, the night was quiet, the street empty except for a black truck idling a block away. Relief washed over her as she recognized Reese's vehicle. She hurried over and climbed into the passenger seat, the tension in her body easing slightly.

"Is the job finished?" Reese asked, his tone flat, while staring straight ahead.

"Yes. It was easier than I thought," Trinity replied with a smile, leaning over to kiss him. For the first time in a long while, she felt understood. Reese was her match, someone who saw her for who she really was.

But her smile faded when Reese's expression darkened. He turned to her, his eyes cold and unforgiving. "Did you fuck him?" he asked.

"No, Why would I do that?" Trinity replied.

"You left the club and didn't say shit. The plan was for you to handle it in one of the private rooms," Reese said, his grip tightening on the steering wheel as he pulled away from the curb.

"I looked for you, but you disappeared. I didn't want to let him get away, so I handled it. Damn, you should be thanking me-"

"You better thank God himself that this shit went as planned. He could've had anybody waiting in that spot! We discussed this shit a thousand times and I told you that NOTHING changes the plan! Reese exploded. His expression daring her to reply.

His words cut through her like jagged glass, each syllable a sharp reminder that the Reese she thought she knew was an illusion. He had never even raised his voice at her before, let alone unleashed this kind of rage. Now, the intensity in his eyes was foreign, cold, and terrifying.

The silence that followed was heavy. Trinity wanted to speak, to defend herself, but the words got stuck in her throat, she was choked by his sudden fury.

Reese's mind raced as he drove. Over the past few weeks Trinity had been both a spark of excitement and a tool for his plans, but cracks had started to form in the picture she painted of herself.

The story she had told him, the name she had given, didn't quite add up. He had tried to dig into her past, but the details were tangled with half truths.

His instincts had been sharpened by betrayal, by family who had turned on him, the cold steel of a prison cell, the weight of years lost, and lessons learned the hard way. He had been burned too many times to ignore the faint stench of deception. And Trinity? She reeked of it. He couldn't put his finger on what it was, but something about her set his nerves on edge, like a song that played just slightly out of tune.

Trinity was a good distraction and a useful asset in the hit on Kahari. But tonight had changed everything. Her decision to go off-script wasn't just reckless, it was dangerous. A flaw too big to overlook. Any fondness he had for her was slipping through his fingers, replaced by a growing distrust that he knew better than to ignore.

He knew he would never love her. That much was clear now. She was heartless, bitter, broken, she was too much like him. Reese knew himself well enough to know that he didn't need any more darkness. He needed balance, light, something pure. But that had been stolen from him years ago, ripped away without warning. The only woman he had ever truly loved was gone, leaving behind a hollow space nothing and no one could ever fill.

The car's tires hummed against the pavement, the sound filling the strained silence. Reese glanced at her out of the corner of his eye. Trinity sat stiffly, her face a mask of quiet defiance and unease. For a moment he considered confronting her, demanding answers about who she really was, but he decided against it. For now, he would watch and wait.

A deep terror clawed its way through Trinity, not just because of the shift in Reese's demeanor, but because of that voice. The one that slithered through her mind like a serpent, whispering cruel truths she could never silence. You're stupid. No one will ever love you. It echoed through her skull, a relentless, sneering companion. You're broke. You're alone. You're nothing. It was the same voice that reminded her of what she could never forget. The same voice that had been commanding her, taunting her, shaping her every decision since she was nine years old. She didn't know if she could handle another loss and realized that the man she thought was her match might be the one to destroy her.

Chapter 9

Rock stood at the edge of the yard, his eyes fixed on Xanae as she laughed and chatted with Shiyah near the pool. The sounds of the cookout filled the air, music thumping from the DJ booth, bursts of laughter from the card table, and the sizzle of meat on the grill. Khi had pulled out all the stops for this gathering. The drinks were flowing, the sun was high, and everyone seemed to be having a good time.

Everyone except Rock. He stayed in the shadows, separated from the crowd, battling the war raging inside him. His eyes traced every movement Xanae made. It drove him crazy how the off-the-shoulder peach sundress that she wore clung to her curves, causing the chiffon fabric to sway over her hips revealing glimpses of her thighs. She was radiant, effortless and utterly unattainable. Rock knew the truth: the feelings eating away at him weren't right. Xanae was Khi's woman, and beyond that, she had become close with Shiyah. To cross that line wouldn't just burn bridges, it would torch every relationship that mattered to him. His partnership with Khi, the money they were making together, his loyalty to Shiyah, it would all be collateral damage. But the more he told himself to let it go, the stronger the pull became. Every time he was in her presence it was like a siren's call. He couldn't help himself, and the thought of risking it all for just one moment with her became harder to resist.

"Nigga, why you over here looking like somebody shot your dog?"

Khi's voice jolted him from his thoughts, as he handed him a cold beer. They were partners and they had business to handle so Khi did his best to keep things cordial. He was sure Rock had taken heed to the warning he had given him.

"Nah, I'm good. Just got some shit on my mind," Rock lied, pulling his gaze away from Xanae. He took a long sip from the bottle, masking his unease.

"You better clear that shit up, man. We got a trip coming up, and I need your head in the game," Khi said, leaning against the fence.

"Trust me, I'm locked in. That's what I'm sitting here thinking about" Rock replied, grateful for the distraction.

Khi nodded, his tone shifting to business. "This Florida spot has to be tight, no mistakes. Everything has been smooth up here, and I want it running just as clean down there. We can't afford slip-ups."

Rock nodded. "It's handled. Ain't no half-steppin." Did you square everything with Cruz?"

"Yeah, I already told him that nothing moves through Biggs without my word. If there's an issue, Cruz knows to bring it to me." Khi said, taking a swig of his beer.

Their conversation was interrupted by a soft, melodic voice that sent a jolt through Rock.

"What are y'all over here scheming about?" Xanae asked, her smile as bright as the summer sun as she and Shiyah approached them.

Khi grinned, wrapping an arm around Xanae's waist and pulling her in for a kiss.

"Talking business, but we're about to start up a card game. What your pretty ass up to?" Khi replied.

"Just trying to figure out who we're spanking in spades this time," Shiyah chimed in with a laugh.

Rock mirrored Khi's move, pulling Shiyah in for a kiss. He forced a smile, masking the bitterness twisting in his chest as he watched Xanae lean into Khi.

"We're about to run to the store for more ice and drinks," Shiyah said.

"Nah, we got it. Y'all stay here," Khi insisted, his tone protective.

"You've been drinking. I don't want you driving," Xanae countered, placing a soft kiss on his lips before turning toward the house.

"We'll be fine, I'm coming Shiyah. Let me grab my purse and find my keys," Xanae called over her shoulder as she stepped into the house. Her sandals clicked softly as she moved through the kitchen.

She checked the counter before heading to the couch, then began pulling the cushions apart, her frustration growing as she continued searching for the keys.

"Damn girl, you would lose your head if it wasn't attached to your body," Shiyah teased.

"Don't do me! Can you check the kitchen again please." Xanae laughed.

Something beneath the couch cushions caught her eye, it was a driver's license. She picked it up, her face screwed as she stared at the name.

"Found them!" Shiyah called from the kitchen. But Xanae barely heard her.

She read the name on the license out loud, trying to make sense of it. ***Nicole Marie Tate.*** Her mind raced. The name was familiar, but she couldn't place it. She studied the picture, the face tugging at a distant memory she couldn't quite grasp. But one thought eclipsed the rest: *Why the hell is this woman's license in my house?*

She stuffed the license into her purse and quickly replaced the cushions.

"Where were they?" Xanae asked, forcing a smile as she took the keys from Shiyah.

"Right on the counter," Shiyah said, studying Xanae's face. "You good?"

"Yeah, I'm fine, let's just go." Xanae replied.

****

When they returned from the store she tried to act normal, but the cookout now felt like a burden. She was no longer interested in the food, music or card games, her thoughts were consumed by the ID burning a hole in her purse. All she wanted was for the guests to leave so she could confront Khi.

Who the hell is Nicole Marie Tate?

Chapter 10

Xanae stared at the laptop screen, her heart pounded in her chest as she read the words in front of her.

Nicole Marie Tate was reported missing by her older sister on July 7th. The 25-year-old was last seen at North East Regional Medical Center, where she worked as a LPN. Coworkers stated that Tate left her shift on the morning of the 6th and was expected to return the next day but never showed. Authorities have been unable to track Tate's phone due to its location services being disabled. If you have any information, please contact the Fulton County Police Department immediately.

She read the article over and over, each word like a puzzle piece clicking into place.

Nicole Marie Tate. The name rolled through her mind continuously. Xanae knew that name. She could see the young woman's face in her memory now, recalling that she was one of the nurses who had been on duty the night she gave birth to KJ. Butterflies danced in her stomach and questions raced through her mind. Had this woman been involved in her kidnapping? What connection did she have to Khi? And why was her ID in their house?

There was no way this was a coincidence. She stood abruptly, causing the chair to scrape across the floor, she quickly headed toward the bedroom where Khi was packing for his trip to Florida. She didn't care if he had a plane to catch, she wasn't letting him leave until she had answers.

When she reached their master suite she paused in the doorway, watching him shove a handful of clothes into his suitcase. Her heart raced at the sight of him, but her anger boiled just beneath the surface.

"What's up baby?" Khi asked, glancing over his shoulder when he felt her presence.

Xanae folded her arms. "You tell me Khi."

Khi's expression changed as he turned to face her. "What's wrong?" he asked, sensing the edge in her voice.

Without a word, Xanae reached into her purse and pulled out the driver's license she had found under the couch cushions. She hesitated, hoping and praying that Khi had an explanation that made sense. But the feeling in her gut told her otherwise.

"Who is this?" she demanded, handing him the ID.

Khi froze the moment he saw it. *Nicole.* His mind reeled as he cursed inwardly. *Where the fuck did she find this?* He thought quickly masking his panic as he handed the license back to Xanae.

"I don't know, where did you find that?" he asked, feigning confusion.

"Under the couch cushions," Xanae shot back, her voice rising. "You told me that you picked out the furniture that was in this house before I got here by yourself. So, tell me this Khi, how the hell did some other woman's ID end up in our brand-new home?"

"Chill out Nae. I don't know that bitch," Khi said, his tone sharp. "You really think I'd bring another woman here? Come on now. That could've come from anywhere Nae, maybe somebody dropped it at the furniture store."

"You expect me to believe that bullshit?" Xanae snapped, stepping closer. Her caramel face blushed from the fire of her fury, her eyes blazing as she glared at him.

"You don't have a choice. The only woman I want is you," Khi said, leaning in to kiss her softly. But Xanae pulled back, shaking her head.

"You not getting off that easy. Not this time Khi. That girl, Nicole? She's missing. And she's not just some random woman. She was one of the nurses on duty when I had KJ. Is that how you met her? Don't lie to me Khi I want the truth."

Khi sighed, running his hand over his face as he searched for the right words. "Nae, you need to calm down. It ain't like that."

"Then what is it like?" Xanae demanded, her voice cracking. "You need to tell me something that makes sense."

Khi hesitated, then relented. "Alright, yeah. I met her that day, but only to put her on payroll. We needed someone who could keep shit quiet if we had medical issues. That's it. Nothing else."

Xanae's voice rose again, filled with disbelief.

"Then why the hell was her ID in our house Khi? Are you fucking her?"

"Damn Nae! No, I'm not fucking her!" Khi shouted, his patience wearing thin. "You tripping. I got a plane to catch, we'll talk about this when I get back."

"No! We're going to talk now, or I won't be here when you get back." Xanae said, her voice cold and resolute.

Khi swore under his breath, his mind racing. He had never intended for Xanae to find out about Nicole, let alone the full truth about Trinity. But there was no more dodging this. He had to come clean.

"Nae, look..... I'ma be honest with you."

"About what?" Xanae asked, her stomach knotting.

"Trinity," Khi said, his gaze dropping to the floor.

Xanae's expression darkened at the mention of her name. Trinity. The woman who had kidnapped her, killed her best friend, and shattered her sense of safety. They hadn't spoken of her in months.

"I didn't know the full story about her not being my sister until after I tried to save her." Khi admitted. "You were unconscious, and she was bleeding out. I just reacted. I brought her here, and I hired Nicole to take care of her."

Xanae's jaw dropped. "You brought her here? To *our* home? The same woman who took us through hell for the past year?" Xanae questioned.

Khi raised his hands in defense. "I didn't know everything then! All I knew was that she was my little sister, or so I thought. I didn't want to let her die, but now I know the truth. And Nicole? She's dead Nae. I found her in the bathroom, and Trinity was gone. Nobody has seen or heard from her since." Khi explained, hoping that Xanae would understand his reasoning.

"You're sorry?" Xanae shouted, tears brimming in her eyes. "She kidnapped me Khi. She killed my best friend, she killed Harmony and pretended to be her! Now she knows where I live. Where my son sleeps! You think your raggedy ass apology fixes that?"

"Nae, listen. She's not coming back." Khi said, trying to sound confident.

"You don't know that Khi! But I do know one thing, I'm not spending my life looking over my shoulder because of her."

Xanae grabbed her purse and stormed out of the room, heading for KJ's nursery. Khi watched helplessly as she lifted their son from his crib, her eyes cold with determination. She didn't say another word as she walked out the front door, leaving him standing there with the weight of his mistakes crushing down on him.

Chapter 11

When Khi and Rock stepped out of the baggage claim at Miami International Airport, they were met with a black Range Rover waiting to pick them up. When the door opened Khi expected to see Biggs, but instead Jade sat casually in the passenger seat, her eyes immediately locked onto Khi.

Jade smiled, her lips curving into a grin that hinted at mischief. “Long time no see stranger.”

Khi nodded briefly, his gaze avoiding hers as he tossed his bag into the trunk and climbed into the back seat. He had made a decision long before stepping foot in Miami that Jade was too tempting, too dangerous. He wasn’t about to let her jeopardize what he had with Xanae.

“What’s up, Jade?”

Rock said as he slid in on the passenger side, oblivious to the tension.

"Nothing much, just thought you gentlemen would enjoy a familiar face," she replied casually. Her eyes flicked to the rearview mirror, seeking Khi's reflection. She blew out a breath, disappointed that he wouldn't look up.

The ride to Bailey Manor was filled with small talk between Jade and Rock. Khi stared out the window, his mind elsewhere. When they finally pulled up to the sprawling estate, he was out of the car before Jade had a chance to speak to him again. He was only focused on one thing! He had to get through this business trip, handle things with Biggs, and get back home to Xanae. Staying in Biggs' home was not his choice, but the man had insisted, and Khi wasn't one to disrespect a host.

"Khi! Rock! Whaa gwan, my youth!" Biggs greeted them at the front steps, his arms open wide, a fat cigar clamped between his teeth.

"Nothing much man, just ready to get this money," Khi said, shaking Biggs' hand firmly. Rock followed suit, the camaraderie between the three men obvious as they headed inside.

"TRUTH!! Biggs replied, his thick Jamaican accent rolling over the words like a wave. "Gwan and make ya self comfortable. We'll talk after you settle in."

Biggs nodded to his butler, who led them upstairs. Khi sighed heavily when he saw the room, specifically the Jack-and-Jill bathroom. He immediately locked the bathroom door and threw himself onto the bed, exhaustion pulling at his body.

He had tried calling Xanae dozens of times, but each call had gone straight to voicemail. The silence between them chipped away at him, each unanswered call and ignored message carving deeper into his soul, leaving a hollow ache that no distraction could soothe. Her absence was like a heavy stone in his chest, and the message she had sent earlier only made it worse. She was cold and distant; he constantly replayed her words in his mind. She said she needed time apart. Time apart? After everything they had been through. He stared at the ceiling, his thoughts churning until sleep finally claimed him.

▪▪▪

When Khi opened his eyes, the first thing he saw was Jade standing over him with her arms crossed and a faint smirk on her lips.

"Hello sleepyhead" she teased, sitting on the edge of the bed like she belonged there.

Khi sat up abruptly, creating space between them. "Jade? You in here watching me sleep and shit?" he asked, his tone sharper than intended.

"I just came to tell you that they're waiting for you downstairs, but since you're avoiding me, I guess you would've preferred someone else to deliver the message." Jade replied, her expression was neutral, it was almost as if her body and eyes were screaming his name but her mouth was saying something different.

Khi ran a hand over his face, his annoyance was clear. "It's not like that Ma. I like you, we vibe, and you don't need me to tell you that you're beautiful. But I can't mess up what I have at home."

Jade’s eyes flashed with a hint of anger, and determination. She stood gracefully, her smile subsiding. “We’ll see,” she said simply, turning on her heel and walking out. She was still bitter from losing West and didn’t care about anyone else’s happily ever after, she wanted her own, she wanted what had been stolen from her.

Khi watched her go, shaking his head. It was clear that she wasn’t used to being told no. He got up, splashed cold water on his face in the bathroom, then made his way downstairs.

“Damn, nigga its bout time Rocked joked when Khi finally joined them.

“My bad Fam” Khi replied dryly as the three men piled into an Infiniti QX80 and headed to the building Biggs had chosen for the operation.

Twenty minutes later they arrived at a huge vacant warehouse with potential written all over it.

"Damn. This is a big-ass space for your first spot," Khi remarked as they walked toward the entrance.

"Why you tink dey call me Biggs? Big man like big tings," Biggs joked, his laughter echoing in the empty space as he led them through the building.

As Biggs outlined his plans, Khi silently assessed the operation. Biggs wasn't just another dealer, he was meticulous, ambitious, and dangerous. Khi reminded himself that Biggs wasn't his subordinate; they were partners. But that partnership came with risks. Cruz's warning echoed in his mind: *once you increase your order, there is no going back.* Biggs wanted 250 keys a month, which was almost triple compared to Khi's previous shipments. If Biggs slipped up, Khi would bear the brunt of it.

They wrapped up the tour of the spaced then headed back to Bailey Manor. Biggs and Rock chatted and laughed with a blunt in rotation, while Khi stared out the window lost in thought. Xanae's words haunted him: *"I think we need some time apart."* He had read the message so many times the words were burned into his memory. The idea of her walking away after everything they shared felt like a knife to the gut. How could he stop now? The money was too good, the power too intoxicating. Even if he wanted to walk away, it was too late. He wasn't just in the game; he *was* the game.

As the truck pulled into Biggs' estate, Khi was clear about one thing- when he got back to Georgia, he was going to get his woman back.

After smoking six thick blunts filled with exotic Kush and drinking damn near an entire bottle of Tequila Khi finally tapped out. Biggs and Rock were still downstairs indulging in their vices: weed, liquor, and women, but Khi had reached his limit. For them it was pleasure; for him it was a desperate attempt to escape the ache of his fractured relationship with Xanae. The haze of smoke and the burn of alcohol couldn't dull the guilt or clear the chaos in his mind.

He stumbled up the grand staircase, his steps heavy with exhaustion. Once inside his room, he locked the door, peeled off his slacks, shirt, and tie, and headed straight for the bathroom. The sound of the water pounding against the tiles echoed in the space, drowning out his thoughts. Khi stepped under the hot spray, closing his eyes as the water streamed over his body, loosening muscles knotted from weeks of stress.

For a brief moment, he exhaled deeply, allowing himself to let go. But peace was fleeting. The memories flooded back, the sting of Kay's death, Xanae's threat to leave him, and the haunting uncertainty of Trinity's whereabouts. All of it piled on top of the pressure of building his empire. It was too much.

The soft sound of the shower door opening pulled him from his thoughts. Khi's eyes popped open, and there she was. Jade stood beneath the running water completely naked. Her ebony skin glistened under the droplets, her curves like something sculpted from marble. Her small perky breasts and tight waist led to hips that seemed to dare him to touch them. Long, toned legs completed the picture, and Khi couldn't help but stare.

"Jade?" What the fuck are you doing? You gotta go." Khi warned her, completely shocked by her boldness.

She didn't answer. Instead, she stepped closer, her body inches from his as the water poured over them both. "Shhh," she whispered, her voice low and sultry. "It will be our little secret, I promise. Just... relax." She said as she began to softly kiss his chest, sending a ripple of heat through his body. Khi knew he should push her away, leave, do *anything* but give in. He tried but the alcohol, and weed he had indulged in earlier, mixed with the sensation of her touch made it damn near impossible.

Before he knew it, her tongue was tracing a slow path down his torso. He moaned as she took him into her mouth, her movements delicate and tantalizing. He bit his bottom lip as his hand tangled in her wet hair. His mind screamed stop but his flesh betrayed him, leaning into the pleasure she offered.

"Fuck," he muttered as his head tilted back against the shower wall.

Minutes later, he carried her to the bed, water still dripping from their bodies. Jade bit his shoulder as he entered her slowly, her nails digging into his back as her legs wrapped around him. The tension that had been simmering between them boiled over, making every touch, every thrust feel electric. She clawed at his skin, her moans muffled as she buried her face against his chest. He didn't think about who he was betraying, in that moment nothing existed but her body and his.

When they both reached their peak, they collapsed against the sheets. Silence filled the room, neither of them knowing what to say, as the reality of their actions began to sink in. The line they had crossed couldn't be uncrossed, and they both knew there was no going back.

Chapter 12

Khi turned the key in the lock slowly, his heart hammered in his chest as he pushed the door open to his home. The house was eerily quiet, void of the sounds that had always made it feel alive. He didn't hear Xanae's laughter or the soft coos of their son. When he stepped inside the air felt hollow, as though it carried the absence of her presence. Khi walked through the house, calling her name, but only silence answered him back. His steps quickened as he headed to their bedroom, hope clinging to him like a fragile thread. When he saw the half-empty closet, her drawers pulled open and bare, the thread snapped.

She was really gone.

His phone felt like a lifeline as he pulled it from his pocket, his hands shaking as he dialed her number. He expected it to go straight to voicemail like it had before, but to his surprise, she answered.

"Hello," Xanae said softly.

Khi could hear the apprehension in her tone.

"Nae," "Where you at?" Khi replied, his heart pounding in his chest.

She hesitated, then sighed. "I found a small apartment for me and KJ. I can't keep living like this Khi. It's too much. I don't feel safe, and I can't keep putting my baby in danger."

"What do you mean you don't feel safe?" Khi demanded. "I would never let anything happen to you or KJ. You know that."

"I know you would die trying," Xanae said quietly, the pain in her voice cutting through him. "But that's the problem Khi. I don't want you to die. Trinity is obsessed with you, she's dangerous and you're still knee deep in the Game. I have to separate my self from all this bullshit Khi. I don't want KJ growing up around this. I love you, but I love myself too, and I have to think about my son first."

"Our son!!! Nae, listen to me," Khi began, desperation creeping into his voice. "I'll handle Trinity. I'll hire security, whatever it takes. I'll make it right, but you can't be out there alone with KJ. You need to come home."

"No," Xanae said firmly. "I can't. This isn't about fixing things anymore Khi. It's about me! I have to do what's best for me and KJ. Honestly, I should've walked away a long time ago, but I thought there was a light at the end of the tunnel. I just.... I can't. I love you, but I can't." Xanae cried as she poured out her feelings.

"Nae I love you and KJ more than anything in this world. You can-"

"I love you too, but love isn't supposed to feel like this. Goodbye Malakhi."

The line went dead, and Khi stood frozen, the phone still pressed to his ear. He had always believed he could have it all- money, power, and love, but now he realized that was easier said than done.

Khi sat alone in his lavishly decorated living room, staring blankly at the textured walls, Italian leather furniture, abstract art, and Persian rugs. The extravagance surrounding him meant nothing. Xanae and KJ had been gone for nearly a month, and every day without them felt like a slow, torturous death.

He met Xanae every few days at the park or a restaurant so he could see KJ, but truthfully it wasn't enough. He wasn't just there for his son, he needed her. Xanae was the air in his lungs, and without her he was slowly slipping away. He knew it was his fault. He hadn't protected her the way he had promised. He had lied about Trinity being dead and despite his love for her, he couldn't walk away from the game yet.

His obligations to Cruz were ironclad, his empire too intertwined with dangerous connections to unravel overnight. He had considered running, liquidating his assets, and disappearing with Xanae and KJ to an island miles away. But men like Cruz had a reach that extended far beyond state lines. Khi knew there was no escaping unless it was on Cruz's terms. The only solution was to play smart, stack his money, and secure a replacement that Cruz would accept. The only problem was that plan would take time, at least a year, maybe more. The thought of living without Xanae until then was unbearable.

He grabbed his keys off the coffee table and left the house, his mind was made up.

Thirty minutes later Khi pulled into the lot of the modest apartment building where Xanae was staying. The neighborhood was clean and quiet, but the sight of it only fueled his frustration. She hadn't even told him where she was living. He had only found out because he had one of his street soldiers following her daily. He hated that she felt the need to hide, that she thought she was safer without him.

He stepped inside the building and immediately noticed the security desk near the entrance. A young, pale security guard sat behind it, looking more like a college freshman than someone capable of handling trouble.

"Can I help you sir?" the guard asked.

"I'm supposed to meet my friend here, but I forgot her apartment number. My phone died so I can't call her, can you tell me which unit Xanae Pittman is in?" Khi said, forcing calm into his voice.

The guard's eyes darted nervously. "Uh, I'm sorry sir, I'm not allowed to give out that information."

Khi leaned against the counter, his voice dropping an octave. "Listen my man, I'm not here to hurt her, I can promise you that. She's expecting me and I need to see her now. I know you have access to a spare key, so just grab it for me and I'll be out of your hair." Khi said as he pulled a thick stack of cash from his pocket and peeled off twenty-five 100-dollar bills, placing them on the desk in front of the Guard.

"You can take this and make it easy, or you can make me do this the hard way. Either way, I'm getting what I came for." He snarled.

The guard hesitated, looking around nervously before grabbing a key ring from a drawer beneath the desk. He handed Khi the key, then reached for the cash.

Before the guard could take it Khi firmly grabbed his wrist. "Thank you, but next time be careful who you sell to the highest bidder" he said, locking eyes with the young man. He didn't need to say more. The guard's pale face turned bright red, and he nodded quickly.

When Khi reached the 11th floor he stopped outside unit 1175, the number that was etched on the key tag. He stood there for a moment listening, unable to hear anything. Slowly, he slid the key into the lock and turned it.

As the door creaked open the scene before him hit him like a sucker punch to the gut.

Rock was sitting on the couch, KJ perched on his lap giggling as Rock played with him.

"Muthafucka, you better start explaining," Khi growled, his nine already drawn as he stalked toward Rock. With his free hand he snatched KJ from Rock's grasp.

Rock stood slowly; his hands raised in a gesture of surrender. "Yo, chill man. It ain't what it looks like. I was just checking on them. That's it, I swear."

"Checking on them?! Nigga you chilling at my woman's crib, playing with my son, and you call that checking in? You knew where she was this whole time and didn't say shit? Something ain't adding up."

"Khi, what are you doing here?" Xanae's voice rang out from behind him. Khi turned to see her standing in the hallway, her hair wet and dripping, a towel barely clinging to her body.

The sight of her only poured gasoline on the fire burning inside him. "Nae are you fucking this nigga?" Khi barked.

Tears welled in Xanae's eyes as she shook her head. "No Khi! It's not like that, I promise! He was just watching KJ while I took a quick shower. Baby, please calm down." She cried.

She reached for KJ, cradling him protectively as she disappeared into the bedroom to lay him down. Khi immediately turned his rage back to Rock.

"You out here checking on MY family huh? You think I don't see the way you been looking at her? I told you from day one- that's all me." Khi spat as he closed the distance between them, his chest brushing Rock's.

Rock stood firm! He wasn't intimidated by Khi, he stared at him without blinking, then took a slow step back.

"Man, you tripping, I told you I was just looking out. It ain't shit but friendship between us. Back the fuck up!".

The air between them was charged with a volatile energy, a challenge that neither man was willing to back down from.

The defiance in Rock's tone was enough to push Khi over the edge. His fist flew, landing a brutal right hook to Rock's temple. The impact sent Rock stumbling into the bookshelf, but Khi didn't stop. His fists rained down on Rocks head as punch after punch landed against his skull, followed by a devastating kick to his midsection.

"Khi, stop! Please, stop!" Xanae screamed as she grabbed his arm, trying to pull him off Rock.

Khi huffed as he stared at her coldly.

"Stop? You defending this bitch ass nigga now? Huh?! I gave you everything, and this is how you repay me? Fuck you Nae. You dead to me Bitch." He spat!

Xanae gasped, Khi had never called her out of her name before. She watched him as he stormed into the bedroom and grabbed KJ.

"Khi, no! Please, don't take my baby! I swear it's not what it looks like. Please!" Xanae's sobs were desperate as she clung to him, her hands grasping at his clothes.

Khi didn't look back. He left the apartment with KJ in his arms, and her cries echoing behind him.

Khi paced the room, rocking KJ gently, as he tried his best to stop him from crying. Exhaustion clawed at every inch of him, his patience wearing thin as he whispered soothing words. "Hush lil man, it's okay. Daddy's got you."

The words felt useless. KJ's wails only grew louder, echoing off the walls of the house.

It had been two weeks since he'd taken KJ from Xanae, and each day without her felt like a punishment he refused to admit to himself. She had called hundreds of times, her voice cracking with desperation as she begged him to bring their son home. Her tears haunted him, but his pride wouldn't let him relent. The image of Xanae with Rock played over and over in his mind, fueling his anger. He couldn't shake the belief that she had betrayed him. They both had.

KJ's cries were a mirror of Khi's own turmoil. He hadn't realized how hard it would be to be a full-time father, especially alone. The pain of his broken family was killing him, yet he stubbornly refused to let Xanae back in.

The sudden ring of the doorbell jolted him from his thoughts. Khi froze, his instincts on high alert, because no one came to his place unannounced. His gut told him it was Xanae, finally deciding to show up instead of calling. Taking a deep breath, he adjusted KJ against his chest and strode to the door.

Peering through the peephole, he blinked in surprise. It wasn't Xanae.

"Jade?" he said, as he slowly opened the door.

She stood there staring at him with those eyes, her flawless cocoa-brown skin glowing, with her hair pulled back into a long soft ponytail.

"I know you must think I'm crazy, but I really need to talk to you. Is now a good time?" she asked.

"Nah, not really," Khi replied, he was guarded and taken back by Jades unexpected visit.

"I'm trying to calm my son down. How you just gonna show up to my crib like this? What if my woman had answered the door?" He asked.

Jade didn't flinch. She just gave him a slight smile, one that could disarm even the coldest man.

"Then I would've told her I was here on business for my uncle. Simple." Her gaze shifted to KJ. "Awww, look at him. He's adorable. Looks just like you. Can I hold him?" She asked, extending her arms.

Khi hesitated. The audacity of her showing up unannounced threw him off, but her presence was oddly comforting. Against his better judgment he handed KJ to her and stepped aside, allowing her to come in.

The moment Jade held KJ his cries ceased, his tiny hands reaching for her face as if he had known her all his life.

Khi blinked, astonished. “That’s crazy, I been trying to calm him down for thirty minutes. How the hell did you do that?”

Jade chuckled softly, cradling KJ with a practiced ease. “I used to be a nurse, and I worked on the labor and delivery floor for a while. Sometimes all it takes is a woman’s touch.”

Within fifteen minutes she fed, burped, and changed KJ before laying him down for a nap in his crib. Khi watched her every move, impressed at how effortlessly skilled she was with his son. Her calm, nurturing demeanor filled the house with a warmth it hadn’t felt in weeks.

“I can’t lie, you have the magic touch,” he admitted, leaning against the doorway. “But why are you here?”

Jade's eyes met his, her expression was serious. “I’m going to be honest with you Khi. I can’t get you off my mind." She paused, her fingers fidgeting slightly as if she was unsure of her next words. "I know you have a woman, and I'm sorry for taking things there with you before, but I need closure. I'm not the type of woman who can just hit it and quit it. I feel like if you're going to be doing business with my uncle, we need to establish a relationship. If it's going to be platonic that's fine, but I need to know where we stand so I can act accordingly."

Khi studied her, noting the confidence in her posture and the vulnerability just beneath it. She was bold, no doubt, but something about her sincerity made him pause. She wasn't demanding or playing games, she was just laying it out.

"Damn," you came all the way to Georgia just to find out where we stood?" He asked.

Jade laughed softly. "No, silly. I came to see an old friend. I thought about it all night and since I'm here I knew I had to talk to you. If your woman had been here, this would have been strictly business, no pleasure."

"Well....she ain't here, Probably won't be for a while. Things have... changed." Khi admitted.

"Changed? I hope it has nothing to do with what happened between us." Jade replied.

Deep down, Khi knew he had overreacted. He knew he had no right to stand on a pedestal considering what had happened between him and Jade. Their encounter slept at the edges of his conscience, a constant reminder of his own betrayal. He never planned to cheat on Xanae, never imagined he would cross that line, and swore it wouldn't happen again. Yet, the thought of calling her to apologize felt like swallowing razor blades. His ego wouldn't let him, not when the image of her and Rock together still burned like a fresh wound.

It didn't matter that she swore nothing had happened, doubt still lingered, and it was something he just couldn't ignore. Her supposed betrayal felt bigger, heavier, more personal. His mind twisted logic to soothe his pride. Man math, he thought bitterly, the only way to justify his actions. If he didn't, the weight of his own hypocrisy would crush him. So he clung to the anger, letting it keep the guilt at bay, even as it tore him apart from the inside.

"It doesn't. It just is what it is," Khi replied, brushing off the thought of Xanae. He didn't want to talk about her, didn't want to dwell on the pain. Right now, Jade's presence felt like the escape he desperately needed.

"I guess I showed up at the right time then," Jade said with a seductive smile.

Chapter 13

Jade moved around Khi's kitchen with ease, preparing a meal that filled the house with the rich, savory scent of curry chicken, rice and peas. She plated the food with care, adding perfectly fried plantains and fluffy coco bread, then placed the dishes in front of Khi.

They ate in silence at first, but gradually the tension between them shifted into something more comfortable. As the evening stretched on, they moved to the living room.

The soft flicker of the TV cast shadows across the room as they watched movies, the hum of shared laughter filling the otherwise quiet space. As night wrapped around them Khi leaned back, his exhaustion finally catching up to him. "You can stay here tonight; there's no point in looking for a hotel this late. The spare room is yours" he offered.

Jade hesitated, her lips curving into a faint smile as she studied him. “If you insist,” she replied, something flickered behind her eyes, but Khi couldn’t tell what it was.

As Khi disappeared down the hall, Jade lingered for a moment, glancing around the house that already felt familiar. She settled into the spare bedroom, lying on the plush guest bed, she traced the pattern of the ceiling with her eyes, a quiet satisfaction humming through her chest. Everything was falling into place. She had woven herself into Khi’s life, step by calculated step. The pieces of her plan were aligning perfectly, though no one-not even Khi, suspected the strings she was pulling.

"Hey, baby boy, I missed you” Jade cooed as she tickled KJ’s tiny feet. His little giggles filled the room, and Khi couldn’t help but watch as the bond between them grew. Jade held him in her arms and softly hummed lullaby’s as she paced the floor. The way her hands cradled the baby's delicate frame was almost hypnotic. It had only been a few weeks since she popped up, but the way she cared for his son was hard to ignore.

Jade had slipped into his life like she belonged there, cooking his meals, keeping his house spotless, and effortlessly taking on the role of a caretaker for KJ. She was everything a man could want on paper. Beautiful, sharp, and connected to Biggs, her presence seemed to align perfectly with the life Khi was trying to build. Yet, no matter how much sense it made, his heart refused to let go of the one woman he couldn't seem to have. He swallowed hard, thinking of Xanae. Meeting her at the park earlier to pick up KJ had left a knot in his chest. She looked radiant, even in her simplest outfit, but the distance in her eyes had gutted him. He missed her fiercely. He missed the way her laugh could fill a room, the way her presence made him feel grounded in a world that constantly threatened to spin out of control. But he knew it was more than that. It wasn't just her love he craved; it was her forgiveness and her loyalty.

Khi sighed as he glanced at Jade. She had been a distraction, one that he hadn't meant to let slip this far. As much as he enjoyed her company, he knew he was keeping her at arm's length. His heart still belonged to Xanae, and no matter how hard he tried to convince himself otherwise, nothing was going to change that. A sudden ring of the doorbell yanked Khi from his thoughts. His body tensed, and a wave of unease washed over him. He stood slowly, the air in the room shifting.

"You want me to get that?" Jade asked, her voice sweet and unassuming as she rocked KJ in her arms.

"Nah, I got it. Just watch lil man for me," Khi replied, his voice low as he made his way to the door. His heart raced as he peered through the peephole and saw her. It was Xanae.

He hesitated for a moment, cursing under his breath before unlocking the door. The sight of her always made his knees weak. "Nae? What's wrong? I thought we agreed I would bring him back on Sunday," Khi said, trying to keep his tone even.

"Yeah, we did, but you forgot his diaper bag. I was right up the street, so I figured I would drop it off," Xanae said casually, though her eyes darted around the house. "Where is he?" She asked.

Khi hesitated. "Uh, he's... sleeping," he stammered, trying to shield the truth from her curious gaze.

"Sleeping?" Xanae raised an eyebrow, stepping closer. "You got me standing here like a stranger Khi. You bought this house for me, remember? Let me in boy." She laughed lightly and pushed past him before he could protest.

Panic bubbled in Khi's chest as he tried to think of something, anything to stall her. But before he could, Jade appeared in the living room cradling KJ with a serene smile.

"Is everything okay baby?" Jade asked, her voice dripped with honey, but her words cut through the room like a machete. The sugary tone couldn't mask the sharp glint in her eyes, a look that stayed just a beat too long on Xanae, as if daring her to respond.

Xanae froze, the small polite smile she'd worn like armor was slipping away. Her eyes flicked from Jade to Khi, her face contorting as the realization of betrayal dawned on her. She drew a slow, deep breath before mirroring Jade's words with venom. "Well, *baby,* is everything okay?" She asked mocking each syllable.

Her steps were steady, as she moved forward to take KJ from Jade's arms. Xanae's touch was gentle, but her intent was clear: *This is my son. My family.* Her dark eyes locked onto Jade's, waiting for her to resist. She was more than ready to make a scene.

Jade put on a mask of poise hiding her true feelings, managing a smile before she relinquished KJ without a word, but she didn't flinch, her eyes remained on Xanae, heavy with an unspoken challenge that filled the air like smoke.

"Nae, this is my business partner's niece, Jade, she's just staying with me for-"

"You don't have to explain shit to me Khi! We're not together!" Xanae snapped, cutting him off. Her voice trembled with rage, and she was barely holding it together.

"It's crystal clear where we stand now. I think I'll just keep KJ with me this weekend, since you've got... company."

Xanae didn't wait for a reply, the tension in her shoulders outlined her hurt as she turned toward the door. The sight of Jade still standing there, serene and composed burned in the corner of her eye. As Xanae left, her heart hammered in her chest, but she refused to let them see her falter.

Behind her, Jade's faint smile remained, her eyes following Xanae's retreat like a shadow. She turned to Khi, the look in her eyes was unsettling. There was something about the way she tilted her head, as if every word spoken had gone exactly as she had intended. Something unnervingly deliberate.

Jade's presence felt heavier now, their dynamic thick with implications Khi couldn't quite figure out, but he could feel it. A subtle shift. In the back of his mind he wondered if Jade had already moved a piece on the Chess board that he didn't see.

"What was that?" Khi growled as he spun to face Jade

"What was what?" She asked innocently, though the slight smirk on her lips proved that her actions were intentional.

"Don't play games Jade. You knew what you were doing. Coming down here, holding my son, calling me baby? You wanted to cause a problem."

"A problem?" Jade echoed, her voice rising. "There is no problem with me Khi. The problem is you. We've been together every day for weeks. I've been taking care of your son, cooking for you, sharing your bed, but now I'm just your business partner's niece? Is that all I am to you?" She asked.

Khi's jaw tightened, and he tried to choose his next words carefully. "I like you Jade. But I love her. She's the mother of my child. I can't just-"

"I'm the mother of your child too!" Jade snapped, cutting him off. Her words hitting him like a bomb.

"What?" Khi asked, his voice barely above a whisper. His stomach filled with anxiety as he stared at her, trying to process what she had just said.

"I'm eight weeks pregnant Khi. It's yours and I'm keeping it." Jade said, her voice unflinching.

Khi sank onto the couch, his mind spinning. He felt the room getting smaller "Are you sure? How do you know it's mine?" He asked. He didn't mean any disrespect, but he and Jade had only shared one intimate encounter, one moment of pleasure that might lead to a lifetime of pain.

"I haven't been with anyone else since my husband died. You don't have to believe me now, but you will." Jade replied coldly.

She turned and walked out of the room, leaving Khi sitting in stunned silence. His heart pounded as her words sank in. He thought things couldn't get more complicated, but now, his world had been turned completely upside down.

Chapter 14

Rock exhaled slowly, his chest tightening as he waited for Khi to show up at the warehouse. The tension between them had become a smoldering fire since that night at Xanae's apartment, and though they had managed to keep things professional over the phone, every conversation was sharp-edged and brittle. Both men knew the stakes, money had to be made, but the unspoken animosity between them threatened to crack the foundation they had built together.

The creak of the warehouse door echoed through the dimly lit space, causing Rock to instinctively rest his hand on the cool steel grip of his 9mm. His eyes followed

Khi's stride, noting the way his old friend moved with unshaken confidence, like a predator surveying his territory.

"Khi," Rock said, his tone flat, as he stood his ground.

"Rock." Khi replied, equally curt. He nodded once, then dropped into a chair at the center of the room, his posture relaxed but his gaze was sharp. He waited as if daring Rock to speak first.

Rock hesitated, then moved to the chair on the opposite side, every step heavy with resentment.

"This shit between us ain't working. Since you made the bitch-ass decision to fall for my woman, the only move left is for you to step down." Khi said blatantly.

Rock gritted his teeth as he leaned forward. "Step down? Nigga, are you out your mind? I built this shit. Me.

What I look like stepping down from MY city, my soldiers? I brought you in, I put you on. I'm not going nowhere." Rock said boldly.

Khi let out a short, humorless laugh, leaning back in his chair like a king unimpressed with a subject's defiance. "Your city? That's cute Bitch nigga but check this out. That shit is Dead! Yeah, you had a little something going, a few bricks here and there, but you wasn't running shit! Cruz wouldn't even fuck with you heavy until I showed up. Now this is MY operation, my empire. I'm giving you a choice. You can take the easy way out, or the hard way. It's on you!" Khi retorted.

Rock's hands balled into fists, his nails digging into his palms. "What exactly does the easy way look like?" he asked through gritted teeth.

"I'll buy you out. Two million flat. You take the money, pack your shit, and leave Georgia. Start fresh somewhere else, rebuild if you want. Khi's voice dropped an octave, and he stared Rock square in the eyes. It's simple. If you don't take the deal, it's war. If that's the route you choose to take then cool, but let's be clear- after today, when I see you it's either me or you. Somebody's not walking away."

Rock's pulse pounded in his ears as he stared across the table at Khi. A war meant tearing apart the crew they had built, forcing men to pick sides. He knew some would stick with him, but loyalty only stretched as far as the money lasted, and Khi had the deeper pockets. Two million wasn't enough to soothe the sting of losing his city, but it was enough to start over. The question was, could he swallow his pride long enough to take the deal?

Rock inhaled sharply, weighing his options. "You got my money now?" he asked reluctantly.

Khi smirked, a flash of triumph gleaming in his eyes. "Nah, but you'll have it by the end of the day."

That smug chuckle, the way Khi leaned back in his chair as if he had already won, was a hit to Rocks Pride. He could feel the unspoken taunt: Nigga I'm King. You will never be me.

"Bet," Rock said, rising to his feet. He moved slowly, his body language calm, but beneath the surface, a storm was brewing. He would let Khi think he won, but Rock wasn't about to lay all his cards on the table just yet. He had plans, and when the time came, Khi wouldn't see it coming.

As Rock walked out of the warehouse, he didn't look back. His mind was already turning, calculating his next move. Georgia might not be his anymore, but this wasn't over. Not by a long shot.

Jade stared out the passenger window of Khi's sleek black Benz, her reflection ghosting back at her as the city blurred past. The hum of the engine filled the silence between them, a silence that was filled with words unsaid and truths that cut deep. She rested her hand protectively on her belly, her fingertips tracing idle patterns over the small life growing inside her. This wasn't how she had envisioned things ending or beginning. She felt disregarded and used like an old mattress that you threw out when it was no longer comfortable.

Khi glanced at her, her profile set in stone, her lips slightly parted as if holding back a thousand unspoken thoughts. His hand shifted to her thigh, a small gesture meant to soften the mood, but Jade's body stiffened under his touch.

"Why are you so quiet Jade?" he asked, already knowing the reason for her standoffish demeanor.

"What's left to say Khi? You've made it clear where you stand. I'm just trying to process it." She replied without looking at him.

Her tone was calm, too calm, as she stared out the window, the cityscape giving way to the emptiness of the freeway. For a moment, Khi thought about pulling over, about holding her face in his hands and telling her everything would work out, even if he didn't know how. But he couldn't lie anymore...not to her, not to himself.

"Jade if things were different, if this was another time, another place, you and me? We could've worked, but you know my heart belongs to Xanae. It always has. Shit wasn't supposed to go down like this."

Jade turned her head slowly, finally meeting his eyes, her hurt and anger barely contained.

"Another time, another place?" she echoed, her words laced with sarcasm. "So what? I'm just collateral damage in your love story? Something that just happened? What about our child Khi? Does another place, another time include them too?" She asked, laughing bitterly.

Her words sliced through him, and Khi flinched inwardly. "Jade, it's not like that," he said, his tone strained. "I'm gonna take care of my child. I'm gonna take care of you, but I can't have you here right now. I have a lot of shit going on, and Florida is safer, we both know Biggs prefers you there anyway."

"Biggs?! It's always about business with you, isn't it? Just be honest Khi, you don't want me to leave because you're worried about my safety! You want me to leave for your own selfish ass reasons, and we both know that. Keeping me here complicates your perfect little plans with Xanae. Be honest Khi, what am I to you? A mistake? A burden, a maid or a nanny? Because something shifted suddenly and the bond I thought we were building collapsed as soon as Xanae found out about me."

Khi slammed on the brakes at a red light. Causing them both to jolt forward. "Jade, what the hell do you expect from me," he said firmly, turning to face her. "None of this was supposed to happen, but here we are. You damn near seduced me! I didn't come after you! One night! One moment of weakness and everything changed. Now you're here, carrying my seed, saying you don't want more, but your every move tells me a different story. I'm caught in this storm, trying to do right by you, by this situation. You might not like the choices I'm making, but I need you to trust me, to believe that I'm trying to navigate this the best way I can, for all of us."

"So, I Seduced you? Wow! I guess I was forward, but only because I felt the connection between us! Remember that you had a choice when I showed up at your door. You could've turned me away while you licked your wounds, but you chose to let me in, you chose to deepen that connection that we both know was there from the start! Now you're asking me to trust you, claiming that you're doing the right thing for US? You're making decisions for me and our baby; while trying to mend your relationship with someone else and you just want me to trust you? Khi, you're walking a fine line."

The light turned green, and Khi accelerated. He didn't want to argue. He didn't want to hurt her, but every word out of her mouth was another reminder of how badly he had messed up.

The rest of the ride to the airport passed in silence, the tension thick enough to choke on. Khi's mind raced, replaying every mistake, every lie, every moment of weakness that had led them here. When they arrived, he got out to grab Jade's bags.

"I can wait with you until the flight boards," he offered, trying to bridge the canyon between them.

Jade shook her head, her expression stoic.

"No need," she said as she stepped closer, just near enough that he could catch the faint scent of her perfume. She pressed a kiss to his lips, it wasn't tender, or passionate, but filled with pain, pain from a source that Khi hadn't even realized he had caused.

As she pulled back, she locked eyes with him. "Be careful with me Khi," she whispered before she turned and walked away, her heels clicking against the cold airport tiles.

Khi stood frozen, her words reverberating in his mind. Be careful with me. For some reason he felt like they were a warning, a subtle threat.

He watched her all way, even after she disappeared into the crowd her presence lingered. Something in her tone, in the way she looked at him, set his instincts on edge. He headed back to his car lost in his thoughts. He had done the "right thing," but why did it feel so wrong?

****

Xanae woke up to banging on her door. She glanced at the phone screen glowing beside her bed, it was 1:17 AM. She knew that it was Khi. She thought about ignoring it, letting the banging dissipate into silence. But then, the thought of KJ waking up stopped her. Her son seemed to sense her pain, the little boy hadn't slept through a full night in over a week.

With a reluctant groan, Xanae swung her legs over the side of the bed. Her body protested every movement, as if each step drained what little strength she had left. Two weeks. That's how long it had been since she'd seen Jade in the house that was supposed to be hers. Two weeks of drowning in heartbreak and rejection. She had told Khi they needed time apart, but never in her worst nightmares did she imagine he would move on so quickly, leaving her shattered in the wreckage of their love.

Her phone had been a constant reminder of him. The missed calls, unanswered texts, and voicemails she couldn't bear to listen to. She hadn't left the house in days, except for one trip to get groceries. She dragged herself to the door. Her eyes were barely open, her body limp from weariness. She didn't have the energy to talk, let alone argue with Khi. With a sigh, she unlocked the door, not bothering to open it before turning away. She didn't even look at him. She couldn't. Instead, she shuffled back to her bedroom, craving the sanctuary of her bed. The sound of the door opening behind her was unmistakable, but she kept her back to him, unwilling to let him see the pain etched across her face.

"Khi, I'm tired, I don't want to do this right now. Sleep on the couch. We can talk in the morning." she said, her voice empty.

"Nae stop," Khi said softly, his hand reaching for her arm. His touch was gentle, but it burned, igniting something she had tried so hard to extinguish.

She whirled around to face him. "What Khi?! What do you want from me? You got a bitch at your house right?! The house you said was mine? Take your ass back to her and let me be great!"

"Nae, she's gone! I made her leave. I want you to come home. I need you. I know I've lied. I know I've hurt you. I haven't been the man I promised I would be, but I swear, all of that is going to change."

Her laughter was bitter, it was obvious that she took his words with a grain of salt. "Oh, now you need me? Khi I can't-"

"You have to!" Khi's voice rose, with a force so strong it made Xanae's heart race. His eyes were filled with desperation. “You have to Ma! I can’t- no, I won’t live without you!”

His words hit her like a tidal wave, crashing against the walls she had tried so hard to build. She knew his intensity wasn’t born of aggression, but passion. He wasn’t just speaking, he was pleading, pouring his soul into every word. The worst part was she felt it too. She couldn’t deny that each second without him felt like she was dying, drowning in her own loneliness.

Tears streamed down her face as she stared into his eyes. She wanted to scream, to shove him away, but she couldn’t. She moved toward him like a moth to a flame. He was her poison, slowly killing her, breaking her down until she was nothing. But he was also her antidote, the only thing keeping her alive.

"Khi..." Was all she could manage to say before her voice cracked.

He stepped closer and gently lifted her chin. His lips found hers, and in that moment everything else fell away. She forgot about the hurt, the betrayal, the anger. All that remained was him. She kissed him back, her body and soul surrendering completely.

When they pulled apart, her heart pounded in her chest. She didn't speak; she didn't need to. The decision was already made. She was going back home.

Chapter 15

Trinity lay sprawled across the bed, her body felt weightless, she was floating in a haze that carried her far beyond the grim confines of the hotel room. For the first time in what felt like an eternity, she was at peace. The euphoria coursing through her veins lifted her above the pitfall of her life, making her feel untouchable, invincible. It was as if she were soaring through the heavens, free from pain, free from memory. She never wanted to come down.

When the anxiety attacks started, ripping through her chest like claws, she begged Reese for something, anything to make them stop. When he didn't offer a solution, she found her own. Cocaine had become her salvation. Each line dulled the jagged edges of her trauma and silenced the echoes of her past. When she was high she could forget her horrible childhood, the ghost of her marriage to Dame, and the pain of every miscarriage that had hollowed her out. She could forget the baby she had birthed but never held, her tiny body already gone before Trinity had a chance to breathe her in. She could forget the faces of the people she had killed, the sting of rejection and the emptiness of never being truly loved. In the haze, none of it mattered. She was untouchable. She tried her best to hide it from Reese, but she knew he had his suspicions.

Reese had delivered on his promise of money, but that was just a detail now. Their initial spark has sizzled since the hit on Kahari. She thought about leaving, about starting over somewhere else, but if she left what would she do? Where would she go? She had no other options. No one to turn to. No family to save her from drowning. No friend who would so much as lend her twenty dollars. She had burned every bridge she had ever crossed, leaving her stranded and alone, except for Reese. He was all she had.

The sharp yank of the covers broke through the fog, snapping her back to the fluorescent reality of the hotel room. Sunlight spilled in as Reese threw the blinds open, the light piercing her eyes like shards of glass.

"Get up!" he barked, his voice sharp and commanding. The words pulled her out of her daze.

"Reeeesssee, I'm tired," she whined, dragging the pillow over her face to shield herself from his piercing glare.

"We got money to make," he snapped. I just got a new envelope, and the price tag on this one is bigger than any of the others. But this one ain't gonna be easy to get next to either."

He tossed a stack of photos onto the bed. They spilled across the rumpled sheets like a dealer's hand, the faces and places solidified in black-and-white clarity. Trinity reached for them lazily, but the moment her eyes locked on the images, her body stiffened. The high that had cradled her moments before evaporated, leaving her lucid. Her stomach turned and she started feeling lightheaded, before she could stop herself, she bolted for the bathroom.

The nausea hit her like a wave as she collapsed to her knees, clutching the toilet. Her body heaved, expelling what little was left inside her. Tears blurred her vision as the images in the photos flashed through her head. It was Khi. His face was seared into her mind, staring back at her from the glossy paper. The one person she never expected to see in the envelope.

She clung to the cold, unforgiving porcelain of the toilet. Her body convulsed violently as she released the last remnants of food in her stomach, leaving her weak and trembling. The burn of bile scorched her throat, but it was nothing compared to the turmoil rolling inside her. She pressed her forehead against the rim of the toilet, her breaths shallow as she tried to ground herself to no avail.

The bathroom door slammed open, the sound ricocheting off the tile like a gunshot. Reese's towering frame filled the doorway, his expression dark and probing. "What's wrong with you?" he demanded with suspicion. "Why the hell you throwing up like that?"

Trinity didn't lift her head. She wiped at her mouth with her fingers, avoiding his gaze. "I don't know," she croaked, her voice flat, void of emotion. "Must've been something I ate."

"Nah," Reese said, his eyes narrowing as he stepped closer. "It ain't nothing you ate." He crouched slightly, studying her. "You ain't pregnant, are you?"

The question stole what little breath she had left. She knew Reese wasn't one to ask idle questions. He was piecing things together, and the thought alone made her realize that the possibility of being pregnant was all too real. They never used condoms, and sex was as habitual as breathing for them. But a baby? That wasn't in the cards for her. Not with him, not with the life she was living. Reese's cold eyes told her exactly what he thought, a pregnancy would be nothing but a complication, and complications were something he had no patience for.

Forcing herself upright, she turned to the sink, rinsing her mouth with shaking hands.

"I just need a hot shower and some rest," she said flatly, willing him to let it go.

Reese watched her for a long moment before stepping back. "A'ight," he said curtly, leaving the bathroom.

As the door closed behind him, Trinity let out a shuddering breath and leaned against the wall. She couldn't stop the question from clawing at her mind: who had ordered the hit on Khi? His name alone carried weight, he was big time now, a kingpin whose empire spread wide and cast long dangerous shadows. Enemies were inevitable in a game like his; sooner or later someone was bound to take their shot. But this? Never in her darkest dreams had she imagined that she would play an instrumental role in his demise. How had it come to this? How had she become the weapon pointed at someone who had once felt like a lifeline she had always needed? She turned the water on, stepping into the shower before it could even warm up. The heat slowly enveloped her, but it did nothing to soothe the storm inside her. Khi's face lingered, haunting her. Reese's words echoed in her mind: ***"The price tag on this one is bigger than any of the others."***

Her loyalty was supposed to lie with Reese, but Khi wasn't just another target. There was a connection there, one that wouldn't make sense to a sane person. A bond forged in the fragments of a childhood fantasy. Her dream of finding her long-lost brother had collided with the grim reality of her life. When she finally stepped out of the bathroom with towel wrapped tightly around her, Reese was waiting, his eyes probing her every moment for answers. “You were in there a long ass time,” he said, as she began to get dressed.

“Yeah, I just needed a little time to think.” Trinity replied, trying to keep her voice steady.

“To think about what?” Reese pressed.

She took a deep breath, twisting the truth before she could stop herself. “The mark is my foster brother. We grew up together. I stayed with him and his family for a while when me and my husband were going through it.”

Reese sneered. “Your foster brother? So what? He ain’t blood, and you know the rules. The only exceptions are kids, anybody else can get it. I don’t care if he was your daddy. This hit is going down.”

Trinity nodded, the lump in her throat threatening to choke her. “I know the rules,” she said bitterly. “I just wanted you to know all the details before we go into this. I know how he moves, his house, his woman, his routines. You said he wouldn't be easy to get close to, but I can make it easier."

Her voice was calm, measured, but inside, she was crumbling. Guilt and dread tore at her, relentless and unyielding. She had made her choice, a decision that felt like stepping off the edge of a cliff into an abyss. But as she continued to think about what would come next, one thought nagged her: when the moment came, could she really pull the trigger?

Chapter 16

Xanae took one last glance at herself in the mirror, smoothing the delicate fabric of her cream-colored Yves Saint Laurent gown. The dress hugged her curves and flowed effortlessly to the floor, its pristine shade a striking contrast to her radiant golden skin. Her sleek, jet-black ponytail cascaded down her back, framing the sharp elegance of her features. Tonight was Khi's 28th birthday, and everyone who mattered was gathered in the grand ballroom to celebrate him.

The venue was a vision of Royalty. White and gold draped every surface, from the cascading floral arrangements to the gleaming champagne fountains carved into the shape of Khi's initials. The space buzzed with energy and the air was thick with laughter and music. Yet, as Xanae stepped into the room, the noise seemed to hush. Heads turned, conversations paused, and all eyes followed her as she moved gracefully through the crowd. Her presence commanded the room without effort, her beauty and poise unmatched.

Khi spotted her instantly. A slow smile crept across his face as he watched her approach, each step reminding him why tonight was going to be unforgettable. "Happy Birthday baby," Xanae said softly as she reached him, drawing a few envious glances from the circle of men around him.

"Thanks Ma," Khi replied, pulling her close, his arms wrapping around her small waist as he placed soft kisses along her neckline. He inhaled her scent, it was intoxicating, filling his senses, grounding him in the moment. Tonight was about more than just celebrating another year. Tonight, he was making a move that would change everything.

Khi had worked to tie up loose ends, securing his empire piece by piece. Trinity was still a thorn in his side, but he had handled that the only way he knew how. A price was on her head, and everyone in his circle knew that if she dared step foot in Georgia again, she was to be brought to him alive. There were unanswered questions, questions about Harmony, his mother's journal, and truths he wasn't sure he could ever fully uncover. But for now, he pushed all of that aside. Tonight was about Xanae. Tonight was perfect.

Excusing herself, Xanae drifted toward a group of wives and girlfriends gathered near the champagne fountain. She smiled and exchanged pleasantries, but her heart ached quietly. Nights like this made her miss KoKo more than ever. KoKo had been more than a friend; she was a sister, someone who understood Xanae in ways no one else could. Since her passing, life had felt lonelier, and even the glitz and glamour couldn't fill the void. Swallowing the lump in her throat, Xanae tried to focus on the present, letting the sound of the DJ's voice pull her back into the moment.

"Aight, y'all, let's give it up for the birthday boy- Mr. Malakhi Banks himself!"

The crowd erupted into cheers as Khi strode toward the front of the room, exuding confidence in his all-white tailored Tom Ford suit. Under the dazzling lights, he looked every bit like the king he had built himself to be.

"I appreciate all y'all for coming out tonight. Thank you for the love, the gifts, and the energy. Make sure y'all eat, drink, and party, let's make tonight unforgettable! Now, I'm calling my lady up here to help me open a few of these gifts." Khi said, as everyone turned their focus to him.

Xanae laughed softly, shaking her head. It was just like Khi to make his night about her. As she made her way to the stage, the crowd cheered, their eyes locked on the couple. Gift after gift was opened, diamond watches, Cuban cigars, designer scarves, and season tickets to the Hawks Games. Each extravagant gesture spoke volumes about Khi's influence, but nothing could prepare Xanae for what came next.

When Khi reached the second-to-last box, he handed it to her with a sly grin. “Baby, open this one for me.”

Xanae arched a brow but obliged, carefully peeling back the elegant wrapping. “Doesn’t feel like there’s anything in here,” she teased, laughing as she pried the box open. A dozen balloons floated out, shimmering under the lights, and her laughter faded as her eyes caught sight of the 5-carat diamond solitaire tied to the end of the strings. She gasped, her heart racing as Khi dropped to one knee and took her hand.

“Nae, things haven’t been perfect with us, but they’ve always been worth it. The only thing I want for my birthday is to make you my wife. Will you marry me?”

Tears welled in Xanae’s eyes, spilling over as she nodded. “Yes!” she whispered, her voice breaking with joy.

The room erupted into applause as Khi slid the huge rock onto her finger and pulled her into a kiss. The world seemed to blur around them as the crowd shouted congratulations, but Xanae could only focus on the man who had just changed her life.

"Aye, y'all, we got one more gift to open!" the DJ called, motioning toward a medium-sized box wrapped in blue paper with a white bow.

"Shit, I got everything I need right here," Khi said, staring at Xanae.

"Baby, don't be rude," Xanae said, nudging him playfully. "You opened all the others, open that one too."

Khi rolled his eyes with a grin, retrieving the box and holding it up. "I don't see a name on this one," he said, scanning the crowd. "Yo, who's this from?"

Silence fell over the room as everyone exchanged curious looks. Xanae took the box, unwrapping it carefully. Inside was a tiny pink onesie that read, It's a Girl! Her brows furrowed as she held it up, confusion and unease settling in.

"What's this?" she asked, her voice edged with uncertainty as she searched Khi's face for answers.

"Looks like somebody got their gifts mixed up," Khi said, laughing nervously.

"Probably so," Xanae replied, her smile tight as she folded the onesie and placed it back in the box. But her gut twisted, and her instincts told her the gift wasn't a mistake. Still, she refused to let anything ruin the night. She would deal with it later.

"Baby, what's wrong?" Khi asked, his voice cutting through the tense silence as he pulled into the driveway.

The ride home had been quiet, the kind of quiet that felt weird and heavy. This was supposed to be their night; the night they celebrated their engagement and prepared for their happily ever after. Instead, it had turned into something he couldn't quite grasp, leaving a coldness between them he hadn't anticipated.

"Nothing. Why?" Xanae replied, staring straight ahead, not bothering to look at him.

"Because I know you," Khi said, his tone soft but probing. "You haven't said more than two words since we left the party. What's up? You don't like your ring?"

Xanae exhaled and turned to face him, "I love it. But I wanna know it was given in honesty."

His hands tightened on the steering wheel, the words slicing through the air like a blade. "What you mean by that Nae?"

“I’m just saying, if you have something you need to tell me, you need to tell me now. I can’t take any more secrets or lies. If we’re gonna do this, we’re gonna do it right.” Xanae replied.

Khi took a deep breath, clenching his jaw as he stared out into the darkness. He knew this moment was coming, he had known from the second he slid that ring onto her finger. He should have told her about Jade before the proposal, but he couldn’t bring himself to risk her answer. Not then, but now he knew that there was no avoiding it.

“Look Nae, there are some things we need to talk about. Things you’re not gonna like. But I need you to promise me something first, promise me that you will hear me out before making any decisions about us.”

"Okay," Xanae replied reluctantly, her arms folding across her chest as she prepared to exit the car. Her stomach twisted into tight knots, dread creeping into her veins. She prayed silently, begging the universe that whatever Khi had to say wasn't as bad as she feared.

The moment they stepped inside, Khi reached for her, pulling her into a kiss. His lips pressed against hers urgently, trying to convey what his words couldn't. He needed her to know how much he loved her, how much he wanted her, how much he was trying to make this work. But the moment was shattered by the sound of slow, deliberate clapping and a low chuckle that sent ice down his spine.

"Congratulations!" Jade's voice rang out with mockery as she stepped into view, a smug grin plastered across her face.

Khi spun around, his anger and surprise apparent "Jade? What the fuck are you doing here?" His tone was sharp, almost a growl.

"I came to tell you happy birthday Daddy," Jade replied with one hand resting on her growing belly. "Did you get my gift? It's a girl!" Her eyes gleamed as she locked them on Xanae, her grin widening.

The room seemed to tilt, the air sucked out entirely. Xanae's gaze darted from Jade to Khi, her stomach lurching as realization hit. "It's a girl?!" she snapped, her voice trembling with a mix of fury and disbelief. "Khi, what the fuck is she talking about?!"

"Nae, listen-" Khi started, stepping toward her, his hands raised in surrender.

"What the fuck is she talking about?!" Xanae shouted again, kicking off her shoes and yanking her earrings out.

"Nae... baby, look. I was gonna to tell you. I promise I was, but not tonight. Please, just chill," Khi pleaded, his voice strained as he tried to reach for her.

"Chill?!" Xanae laughed bitterly

"You want me to chill? Khi, just tell me she's lying. Tell me this ain't what I think it is, and I'll calm down. That's all I need! Just tell me!" She cried.

Jade leaned against the arm of the couch; her smirk unwavering. "You guessed it," she said with a singsong tone. "Congratulations! You're gonna be a stepmom."

The words were gasoline on an already raging fire. Xanae lunged at Jade, but Khi caught her mid-air, pulling her back as she cursed and turned her punches towards him.

"Bitch, you better shut the fuck up! This is my life! This ain't a game!"

"Baby, calm down," Khi urged, struggling to hold her as she thrashed in his arms wildly, landing hits to his face and head in the process. "It's not like that, I swear!" He said, still trying to calm her down.

"See, that's the problem," Jade cut in. "You're just not cut out for this life honey. Khi needs a real woman, not a little girl who throws a tantrum every time something doesn't go her way."

"Fuck you!" Xanae spat, her voice raw with fury. She finally twisted out of Khi's grip, shaking her head as she stared at him with eyes that burned with betrayal. "This is your problem Khi. Get this bitch out of my house before I make it mine." Without another word, she stormed upstairs, slamming the bedroom door behind her.

Khi balled his fist, as he turned to Jade, his patience gone. "What the fuck are you doing here? How did you even get in?" He asked.

"You gave me a key, remember?" Jade replied, shrugging like it was the most obvious thing in the world. "And I never gave it back. Anyway, I wanted to let you know we're having a little girl. I thought you would like to hear it in person, I didn't mean to ruin the party Daddy."

He rubbed a hand over his face, frustration radiating off him. "Jade, you can't do this. You can't just show up like this. Me and Xanae are back together. I proposed to her tonight! I told you I'm gonna be there for the baby, but we need boundaries. Hand over the key. I'll set you up in a hotel, but you gotta go. Tonight."

Jade grinned as she walked around the room. "A hotel? No, I think I'll stay here. You have a guest room, don't you?"

"You gotta be out of your fucking mind," Khi hissed. "You can't stay here. Get your shit, and let's go."

"Hmm. Maybe I should just call my uncle and tell him the father of my child just beat me up and tossed me out in the middle of the night to make his fiancé happy. What do you think Biggs will have to say about that?" Jade asked.

Khi froze, and took a deep breath, trying to choose his words carefully. "I didn't touch you, and you know it. Whatever dealings we have don't involve Biggs. Keep him out of this."

"Then where's that guest room?" Jade asked, her voice dripping with false innocence.

Reluctantly, Khi's shoulders sagged. "Upstairs. Third door on the right. But don't even look at Xanae."

"Thank you Daddy," Jade said, sauntering off with a victorious smile.

As Khi watched her disappear up the stairs, his stomach filled with a sickness words couldn't explain. He knew that he had fucked up Big Time! This wasn't how the night was supposed to go. Now, he had to figure out how to keep Jade and Xanae from killing each other before he could fix the mess he had made. He was walking into a storm, and he braced himself for the destruction it would bring, but tonight, he didn't have a choice. His hands were tied. He needed to handle Jade, and to do that, he had to talk to Biggs face to face. If he let her manipulate the situation before he could explain himself, it would ruin more than his relationship with Xanae. It would destroy his standing with

Biggs, and that would send ripples all the way to Cruz, a ripple effect that could end in blood.

Taking the stairs two at a time, he tried to think of something, anything, that could soften the blow of explaining why Jade was still in their home. He knew that there was no escaping the truth. The only way out was through. He pushed open the bedroom door slowly, his heart pounding as he stepped inside.

Xanae sat on the edge of the bed, her posture rigid. She stared blankly at the wall. She looked like a woman frozen in time, but Khi knew better. Beneath her stillness was thunder.

"Nae," he said softly, taking a seat beside her, the mattress sinking under his weight.

She didn't turn to look at him, didn't flinch.

"I'm just trying to figure out where the fuck I went wrong." She said, letting out a humorless laugh that sent a chill through him. "One minute, I'm living a normal life, taking college classes, dealing with that fuck nigga Dame, partying with my best friend. You know, regular-ass shit. The next, bitches are trying to kill me, KoKo is dead, and somehow my fiancé has a bitch pregnant... and she's chilling in my living room. This is some real made-for-TV shit, ain't it?"

She began to laugh hysterically, but Khi didn't dare join her. He sat in silence, knowing anything he said would only feed the fire. Instead, he waited, letting her words settle between them.

"Nae, I know you tired of hearing me say it, but I really am sorry." He leaned forward, resting his elbows on his knees, his hands clasped tightly as if he were about to pray. "I wanted to make things right. You gave up on me.

You weren't taking my calls, you moved out, and I... I slipped up." He exhaled sharply, running a hand over his face. "I had no intention of getting her pregnant. The shit just happened. I don't want her, I never did. I want you. That's why I put that ring on your finger tonight. I told you Ma... shit between us ain't perfect, but it's worth it. We can get through this together."

"Together huh?" she said, her voice heavy with exhaustion. She shook her head, refusing to meet his eyes. "Khi, at this point, I'm not even hurt anymore. I'm just tired. Tired of all of this. The one thing I could always say about us is that I never had to deal with you and other females. And I know this happened when I left, but that doesn't make it okay. She was in our house, violating our space, just like that bitch Trinity."

"I know, and I checked her on that shit. As soon as I get the chance to talk to Biggs face to face, she's gone." Khi said quickly, pleading as he leaned toward her.

Xanae's head snapped up, her brows furrowed. "Biggs? What does he have to do with this?"

Khi hesitated for a moment before answering, knowing how bad this was going to sound. "He's her uncle Nae. She's trying to use that as leverage to get me to do what she wants."

Xanae's face twisted with disbelief!

"Her uncle? So, you're telling me every time your ass was in Florida, you were with that bitch?" She yelled.

"No!" Khi protested, his voice rising defensively. "It wasn't like that. It's not like that. I've only slept with her once, I was drunk and trying to process the shit we were going through. Look, I'ma straighten this shit out. But for now, I need you to stand still while I do. She's staying in the guest room for a few days, just until I can get this handled. This weekend, I'll take a flight to Florida, and you won't have to worry about her anymore. I'll take care of the baby, and that will be that."

Xanae stared at him, her expression cold as ice. "That I'll be that!? Khi, you got the right idea but the WRONG woman for this bullshit! I know you're not telling me that she's still here and I'm just supposed to accept that your side bitch is down the hall, sleeping in our guest room? You must take me for a fucking fool." Xanae said in disgust.

Khi opened his mouth to respond, but before he could get a word out, Xanae shot up from the bed, pushing past him with enough force to make him flinch. Her steps were quick and angry. Khi watched helplessly as she disappeared into the bathroom, slamming the door so hard behind her the walls shook.

For a moment, the only sound in the house was the pounding of his own heartbeat. He let out a heavy sigh, dragging his hand down his face. He knew she wouldn't take this well, but this reaction cut deeper than he expected it to. Still, as much as he hated seeing her like this, he couldn't back down. Xanae's anger was easier to deal with than the problems Jade could unleash. If things with Biggs and Cruz fell apart, the repercussions would be far worse than a slammed door and the silent treatment.

He glanced towards the Guest room knowing Jade was probably reveling in the chaos she had caused. His stomach twisted at the thought, but he couldn't dwell on it. Right now, his only priority was keeping the two women from killing each other before he could get Jade out of the house for good.

Chapter 17

Rock scanned the street as he approached the entrance of the police station, every nerve in his body was on edge. His decision pressed against his conscience like a loaded gun. The thought of being here, of crossing this line, sent a bitter taste to the back of his throat. He never thought he would stoop to being a snitch, but in his mind, this wasn't betrayal. This was justice. An eye for an eye. Khi had taken everything from him, and Rock had no intention of letting him walk away unscathed. Retaliation was the only way forward.

"Excuse me, ma'am. I'm looking for Detective Julius Connelly, I believe he's in the Homicide Division," Rock said, his tone even, though his eyes darted over the rim of his dark sunglasses to gauge the officer's reaction.

The female officer looked at him, scanning him with suspicion.

"Is Detective Connelly expecting you?" she asked, remaining professional.

"Nah, but I've got information that could be helpful to one of his cases." Rock replied calmly.

She studied him for a moment before motioning toward the worn plastic chairs lining the wall. "Have a seat. I'll see if he's available." She replied just before she disappeared behind a set of double doors.

Rock eased into one of the chairs, his foot tapping against the floor as the seconds crawled by. Twenty minutes passed, each one stretching his discomfort to its limit. The air inside the station was muggy, and stale but the environment felt sterile. He was a major player in Georgia's drug trade, and this was the last place he wanted to be. Yet there he was, sitting in enemy territory, with a bag full of secrets that could bring everything crashing down. He didn't plan to stick around long, just long enough to hand off the package and disappear.

Just as Rock was about to second-guess his decision, the door swung open. A tall, broad-shouldered Black man stepped out; his suit crisply pressed. He extended a hand toward Rock.

"Detective Julius Connelly. And you are?"

Rock hesitated, glancing at the hand but refusing to shake it. "I'd rather stay anonymous," he said flatly. "But I have got some information, valuable information, on one of your cases. Can we talk somewhere private?"

Connelly raised a skeptical brow but motioned for Rock to follow. "Valuable information huh? Alright. Let's hear what you've got" he said, leading the way to a small, brightly lit interrogation room.

The moment the door shut behind them, Rock's skin prickled with unease. His pulse quickened, and beads of sweat dotted his forehead. The walls felt like they were closing in on him, and the fluorescent lights buzzed faintly, adding to his discomfort. He had spent three years locked up on a possession charge, and stepping foot into any place associated with the police made his stomach sick. He wasn't there to linger.

"I don't have much to say," Rock said, his voice firm but low as he slid a weathered black book bag across the table. "Everything you need is in there. Do what you gotta do."

Connelly frowned, his hand hovering over the bag. "Why don't you sit down and give me a minute to look inside? I might need more information."

Rock shook his head and stepped back toward the door. "Nah, I'm done here. I'm leaving town but trust me, everything you need to know is in that bag." With that he turned and strode out, ignoring the faint call of Connelly's voice behind him. He knew that he had made a bitch move but this wasn't about honor; it was about payback. Khi was about to learn that betrayal cuts both ways.

Connelly opened the bag cautiously, his brow furrowing as he pulled pictures of a young woman, a woman he was familiar with because he had investigated her case. His eyes lit up, hoping that this was finally a lead on the disappearance of Nicole Marie Tate. He noticed that the bag also held a thick, worn journal. The edges of the pages were frayed, the handwriting inside erratic but legible. As he flipped through, names jumped off the page like landmines: Kay, Trinity, Malakhi Banks. His lips pressed into a thin line as he read further.

"I knew there was more to this story than Banks was letting on," Connelly muttered as he began to read the journal line by line.

Outside, Rock wasted no time peeling out of the station parking lot. He kept his eyes straight ahead as he drove silently.

"What was in that bag?" Shiyah asked from the passenger seat. Her eyes studying his every move. She took in the way his fingers drummed nervously on the wheel. She knew him too well; he had always avoided cops like the plague. Watching him walk into a police station with a bag was beyond suspicious.

Rock didn't take his eyes off the road. "Don't worry about it Shiyah, just know that everything that's about to happen is temporary. We will be back in GA in no time Ma. Trust me."

But even as the words left his mouth, Rock couldn't stop thinking about what he had done. He wasn't sure if this move would give him peace or set off a chain reaction that would spiral out of control.

Jade hummed softly to herself as she sautéed vegetables in a pan, the rich aroma of butter and spices filling the kitchen. She glanced at the oven, checking the steak she had carefully prepared. She had been at Khi's house for 3 days, and while he thought her visit had an expiration date, Jade had other plans. Khi barely spoke to her, his presence scarce during the day as he avoided confrontation. Xanae, on the other hand made her disdain clear every time their paths crossed, her cold glares were sharp enough to cut glass. Jade didn't care. She could hate her, she could stare at her, it didn't matter. In Jade's eyes, they could be sister wives if that's what it took. She wasn't leaving until she finished what she came to do.

This wasn't about Khi anymore. This was about vindication; it was raw and personal. Every moment she spent in the house with them felt like an eternity. She wanted to leave, just as much as they wanted her gone. But now that the truth was in her hands, burning like gasoline on her skin, she couldn't walk away. Not until she watched them fall apart, brick by brick, lie by lie, with her own two eyes. Only then would she feel whole again. Only then would the ache in her chest quiet down.

The thought of the life growing inside her twisted her stomach into knots. Nausea crept up her throat as regret engulfed her entire body. She cursed herself for moving too fast, blinded by charm and sweet lies. She had made a mistake that changed everything, trying to fill an infinite void and now she was stuck in the fallout, choking on the consequences.

The faint sound of footsteps drew her attention, and she glanced over her shoulder, spotting Xanae entering the kitchen.

"Hey wifey. You hungry?" Jade asked with a sly smile.

Xanae eyes locked on Jade like a predator stalking its prey, as she pulled out a chair and sat at the table.

"This is all real funny to you, huh bitch?" She replied dryly. She had thought about leaving days ago but the idea of letting Jade feel like she had won was one that was too hard to swallow.

Jade shrugged, unfazed. "I don't find it funny at all. I really don't understand why you're so upset. Our kids are going to be siblings, so we have to get along. We both got pregnant by the same man, it's life sis. Deal with it." Jade spat.

"Let me tell you something, sis!" Xanae shot back. "You and me? We are not the same. You think I don't know the only reason you're here is because Khi doesn't want you to mess up his business with your uncle? Yeah bitch, he told me. He didn't choose you. He chose me. That's why I have the house, the cars, the money, and the ring. You were a one-time mistake, you got pregnant by default on a drunk night because I told him we needed time apart. You're temporary, and in a few days, your ass will be a thing of the past. Don't worry though, I'll make sure we send you a child support check every month."

Jade turned off the stove and laughed genuinely. "One time? Is that what he told you?" she chuckled, pouring herself a glass of red wine. "Women like you think they have it all figured out, but you don't know shit! You seem a little upset, maybe you should relax. Have some wine. Since you know so much about the situation with my uncle, I'm sure you also know Khi's money is the last thing I need. Deep down, you know I'm here because some part of him wants me to be."

"Girl please." Xanae scoffed, rising from her seat and snatching the wine bottle out of Jade's hand. "Once again, this is my house, my kitchen, Khi is my man, and this is my damn wine." She said, snatching the bottle from Jades hand as she turned to leave the room.

Jade laughed softly, following her as she disappeared up the stairs. No matter how much Xanae tried to deny it, she knew she was getting under her skin. She wanted to destroy anything that Khi had ever loved, and Xanae, with all her fire and pride, was playing right into Jade's hands and she didn't even realize it.

After finishing her plate, Jade moved slowly, taking her time as she climbed the stairs. She crept toward Xanae and Khi's bedroom, peeking inside. The bottle of wine sat nearly empty on the nightstand, and Xanae was sprawled across the bed, her laughter bubbling up like champagne.

Jade smirked. The crushed ecstasy pills she had poured into the wine had done their job. Xanae's inhibitions were long gone, this was Jade's moment to strike.

"What's so funny?" Jade asked, stepping into the room and perching on the edge of the bed.

“Liiiife,” Xanae slurred, her words lazy and soft. She sat up, her eyes glassy as she giggled uncontrollably. “Life is funny. I love my life.

Jade brushed a strand of hair from Xanae’s face, her fingers lingered as she leaned in and kissed Xanae’s neck. Jade was a seductress by nature, and she planned on using her power to make Xanae hate herself.

“Wait... what are you doing?” Xanae whined, but her hands told another story, as they slid to the back of Jade’s head, urging her to continue.

“Do you want me to stop?” Jade whispered, as she gently parted Xanae’s legs and began to trace delicate patterns along her thighs.

“Mmm, no... don’t stop,” Xanae moaned. The drug had taken full effect, and she was lost in the sensation. Every touch sent waves of electricity through her body, heightening her pleasure to an intensity she had never felt before.

Jade began to lick the inside of Xanae's thighs with precision, savoring the power she held in that moment. She glanced up briefly, a devious smile on her face as she removed Xanae's panties and began swirling her tongue against her clit.

The sound of soft moans filled the room, Xanae's body shook uncontrollably beneath Jade's touch. The tension built and built until it broke, leaving her breathless as she fell back against the pillows, her body spent.

Jade adjusted her dress, a satisfied grin spread across her face as she turned to leave. Now she had leverage with both Khi and Xanae. As soon as she reached the door, she froze. Khi stood in the doorway and Jade wasn't sure how long he had been there.

"Well hello," she purred, sauntering up to him and placing a hand on his chest.

"What the fuck you got going on Jade?" he whispered. Unsure of what he had just witnessed.

"I don't know what you mean. I just wanted to be friends with her" Jade replied innocently.

"Friends? It looks like she passed the fuck out, you gotta go" Khi replied firmly, dismissing her.

"Looks like she did, so why don't you let me take care of that for you." Jade said as she grabbed the bulge in his pants.

"Nah Jade, we can't" Khi said as he moved her hand.

"We can't what?" Jade asked.

His breathing increased as she pressed her body against his, softly biting his bottom lip. For a moment, he froze, torn between his common sense and the pressure swelling in his dick. Before he could stop himself, he gave in.

Trinity began unbuckling his belt, as she slowly kissed his full lips. She noticed that he didn't hesitate or pull away. The scent of Xanaes pussy on her lips and the softness of Jades mouth did it for Khi. Without a second thought he lifted her from her feet in one swift motion. She wrapped her legs around his waist, slid her panties to the side and positioned her body onto his long thick dick. "Ahhhhh" she moaned when Khi entered her.

"Be quiet!" Khi warned as he looked back at Xanae then pressed Jades back against an adjacent wall. Jade obliged and bit his shoulder as he stroked her pussy hard and fast. Adrenaline pulsed through Khi's body as he focused on the vice grip that her walls had on his shaft, while watching for any signs of Xanae waking up.

"Choke me or I'm going to scream and wake her up." Jade said when she noticed that Khi was watching Xanae. Khi ignored Jade and continued to glide her up and down on his dick, all while watching Xanae sleep.

"CHOKE ME OR I-" Jade said louder, gasping as Khi grabbed her throat and begin to squeeze. Her pussy pulsated as he tightened his grip with each stroke. She moaned loudly, wanting Xanae to wake up. As much as she hated Khi, she couldn't deny that the connection they naturally shared was undeniable. Her body reacted to him in ways that it never had, even with all the detest she felt for him. Khi pounded Jades tightness with increased intensity, placing his hand over her mouth as adrenaline pulsed through him. The thought of getting caught somehow made the sex with Jade even better and within minutes he came inside her.

Jade laughed as Khi put her down and shook his head while trying to catch his breath.

"You fuckin wild man. I gotta get your ass back to Florida" he said as he ran his hands over his face and buckled his pants. He didn't know what kind of spell Jade had put on him, but something told him getting her to leave was not going to be as easy as he thought.

Chapter 18

Trinity sat at the small table tucked into the corner of the hotel room, her heart pounding in her chest as she waited. The flickering light of two candles illuminated the spread she had meticulously prepared. Plates adorned with a perfectly seared T-bone steak, mashed potatoes whipped to a creamy perfection, and asparagus with garlic butter. The tiny kitchen had never looked more inviting, but her nervousness dimmed the mood she had tried to create. Her fingers drummed against the edge of the table as the door clicked open.

Reese stepped inside, his presence commanding as always. Trinity watched him, her pulse quickening. He moved toward her with an air of suspicion, as his eyes scanned the room before landing on her.

"What's all this?" He asked, lifting the cover from one of the plates.

"We have a big day tomorrow, so I thought I would cook for you," Trinity said with a shrug, trying to appear nonchalant.

"Since when do you cook?" Reese laughed, as he removed the cover from another plate. The rich scent of steak and mushrooms filled the air, momentarily distracting him.

Trinity forced a small smile, standing to grab two wine glasses. "We're always on the move. When we finally settle somewhere, I'll cook more often." She replied.

Reese eyed her as he sat down. "I can't lie, it looks good, but does it taste good?" he teased as he washed his hands and took a seat before cutting into the steak

"Just eat," Trinity laughed nervously as she poured wine into the glasses. Her hands shook slightly, but she hoped he wouldn't notice.

"You not eating?" Reese asked.

"Nah, I'm not hungry," Trinity replied quickly, handing him a glass and sitting down beside him.

Reese leaned back in his chair, studying her. "You made all this food, and you ain't eating? That's crazy. Sit down and eat some."

"Damn Reese. I was snacking while I cooked," she said, trying to keep her tone light. "I don't feel like eating a full meal."

Reese's noticed her awkward hesitation and his instincts were on high alert. He looked down at the plate of food in front of him and pushed it away.

"Matter fact, take this plate and give me yours. I want you to eat the one you made for me." He said as he slid the plate across the table with a pointed motion.

Trinity's stomach flipped as she forced herself to comply, knowing he would find her refusal to eat suspicious. She slowly picked up a fork and began eating, taking one bite of potatoes, a piece of asparagus, and two bites of steak. Reese didn't take his eyes off her, his scrutiny as sharp as the knife in his hand. Satisfied, he finally began to eat from the plate she had originally made for herself.

"So, how is it?" Trinity asked, as she took a sip of her wine.

Reese cut into the steak, taking another large bite before answering. "It's good, I wish I had known you could cook months ago." he said through a mouthful, his shoulders relaxing as he continued eating. Trinity smiled and sipped her wine as she watched him devour every bite. Her mind was racing with the plan she had spent days crafting. As he finished the last morsel, she stood and grabbed the empty wine bottle.

"I'm gonna take a quick shower, then I have something special planned for you" she said, her voice dropping into a seductive tone.

Reese smirked as he watched her disappear into the bathroom, the door clicking shut behind her. He leaned back in his chair, savoring the after taste of the meal and the wine. "Maybe shawty ain't so bad after all," he muttered to himself, draining the last of his glass.

Thirty minutes passed before Trinity emerged from the bathroom, fully dressed in a hoodie, sweatpants, and sneakers. Reese's face screwed as he stood, his body swaying slightly.

"Damn, took you long enough, why you got on all those damn clothes?" he asked, his voice slurred. He took a step toward her, but dizziness overtook him, and he dropped back into the chair. A sharp pain stabbed through his stomach.

"Ahhhh, I knew your ass couldn't cook. My stomach is fucked up," Reese groaned, trying and failing to stand again.

Trinity's laugh was cold, void of the sweetness she had shown earlier.

"Are you feeling alright Reese?" she laughed, moving around the room, picking up his jewelry, car keys, the box of photos for their next hits, a throwaway cell phone, and a stack of cash tucked under the bed.

“What the fuck did you do to me?!” Reese roared, doubling over as he clutched his stomach. He tried to lunge at her but collapsed to the floor instead.

Trinity stood over him with satisfaction. “You thought I would let you kill the one person in this world who gives a damn about me? You really thought I would just sit back and let it happen?” She said as she delivered a kick to Reese’s back.

Her voice was different, high pitched and almost child like as she began to laugh. “I knew you would be suspicious about dinner. I knew you would switch the plates. You’re predictable Reese. I’ve been smarter than you the entire time.”

Reese’s eyes widened as agony filled him, making speaking nearly impossible. “What... what did you...?” he stammered.

Trinity crouched beside him, her smile dark and triumphant. "You remember telling me you liked mushrooms? How do the poisonous ones taste?"

Before he could respond Reese's body convulsed; his breathing labored as he tried to crawl toward her. Trinity stood, slipping her bag over her shoulder. She didn't look back as he collapsed with a final thud.

Laughing softly, she opened the door to the hotel room and walked into the night, leaving behind the man who she thought was her match. The game was over and this time, she had finally won.

Xanae groaned softly as she swung her legs over the edge of the bed. Her head throbbed, her stomach hurt, and the world around her tilted slightly as she tried to steady herself. Her eyes drifted to Khi, sprawled out on the bed fully clothed, his arm draped limply across the comforter. His breathing was slow and steady, he looked untouched by the drama in their lives. Xanae blinked, confused, she didn't remember him coming home last night.

He hadn't even bothered to undress, judging by his state she knew he must have gotten in late. She hated that he was so comfortable being gone all day, while she dealt with his mistakes.

She stumbled toward the bathroom, her feet dragging across the plush carpet. Grabbing a white hand towel from the closet, she let cool water run over it, then pressed the damp cloth against her flushed face. The sensation made her feel better, she repeated the action a few times, willing herself to shake off the fog clouding her thoughts. She glanced up at her reflection in the mirror as she searched for clarity.

“Damn, why can’t I remember anything?” she whispered. The bathroom light flicked off behind her as she stepped back into the bedroom, her mind spinning.

Her eyes caught a glimpse of the empty wine bottle sitting on the nightstand. She gasped when the fragmented pieces of the previous night snapped into focus, like jagged shards of glass forming a broken mirror. She remembered grabbing the bottle after the heated argument with Jade, then going to her bedroom. Then, suddenly flashes of the night before drowned her. Jade’s face, her hands, the moment they shared.

Her stomach turned violently. What the hell happened? The images felt unreal, impossible, but the truth sat heavy. Her hands shook as she sank onto the edge of the bed, bile rising in her throat. Then it hit her.

"She drugged me…" The words left her lips in a shaky whisper, she was in disbelief. Anger flared within her, as her mind replayed the way Jade had hovered near the open wine bottle in the kitchen. The way she had smiled. It made Xanae's blood boil, she dug her nails into the insides of her palms, disgusted at the memory of her own vulnerability.

Xanae stood abruptly, her body tense with fury as she turned toward Khi. There he was, sleeping peacefully, calm and unbothered as if the world wasn't crashing down around them. She stared at him, every ounce of love she had ever felt for him dissolving in that moment. Their relationship wasn't just flawed, it was poison. Piece by piece, it had broken her.

Her mind raced through the wreckage of their time together: KoKo's death, the brawl with Trinity, the lies, the betrayal. And now, the ultimate insult, another woman pregnant, living in their house, wreaking havoc on what little semblance of peace she had left. A single tear fell down her cheek as she whispered, "This shit is a wrap."

Without hesitation, she pulled her dress over her head and headed for the walk-in closet. She yanked on a pair of jeans, shoved her feet into her favorite Uggs and threw on a hoodie. Determination replaced the pain in her heart as she raced toward KJ's nursery. Xanae's heart pounded as she scooped him into her arms, holding him close and kissing the top of his head.

She moved quickly; but carefully as she tiptoed downstairs. She flicked on the kitchen lights and began to rifle through drawers, searching for a pen and paper. She thought about leaving a note, telling Khi everything, but the thought felt pointless. Words weren't enough. Actions spoke louder, and she had wasted enough time talking.

She slid her engagement ring off her finger, the massive diamond catching the light one last time before she placed it on the counter beside her phone. No calls. No tracking. If Khi wanted answers, he would have to wait until she was ready to give them. She grabbed her purse and keys, slipping silently into the garage. The cold metal of the car seat buckle clicked into place as she secured KJ in the backseat, trying to stop her hands from shaking.

When she got behind the wheel, tears welled in her eyes, blurring the dashboard. She inhaled deeply, forcing herself to breathe. Anger and unanswered questions swarmed her as she pulled out of the garage. She wanted to be as far away from Jade, Khi and that house as she could. She reminded herself that this wasn't the life she wanted and tried her best to stop her tears, but they wouldn't cease, spilling down her cheeks in waves of regret.

Love wasn't supposed to hurt like this, she reminded herself, the words a fragile mantra against her agony. It wasn't supposed to be this hard. She had to find herself again, had to be whole for her son and for her own survival.

As the house faded in the distance behind her, she didn't look back. She focused on the road ahead, the path that would lead her to the one place she could find solace, clarity, and a long-awaited sense of peace.

"Fuckkkkk!" Khi growled, his voice reverberating through the large kitchen as he grabbed Xanae's phone and engagement ring from the counter. Allowing Jade to worm her way back into his life, into his head, was the mistake that kept costing him. And now Xanae was gone.

"Jade! Jade?! Where the fuck you at!?" he yelled with frustration as he stampeded through the house.

Room by room he searched, his steps heavy and frantic. He checked every corner of the downstairs, from the living room to the guest room where Jade had been staying. Nothing. She wasn't there.

He felt helpless, a feeling he hated more than anything. He couldn't even call Xanae, he knew she had left her phone behind to send a clear message that she did not want him to contact her. Every second felt infinite, feeding his mounting panic.

Khi slowly walked back to the bedroom, his shoulders heavy with dread. When he pushed the door open, he froze. Jade was sprawled across his bed like she owned it. She was completely naked, her long legs stretched out, her body a perfect display of temptation.

"You looking for me?" She asked with a seductive smile, spreading her legs just enough to reveal her freshly shaven kitty.

Khi stared at her for a split second. Hypnotized by her voodoo, clouding his better judgment with her boldness. But then reality slapped him, and he forced himself to look away.

"What the fuck are you doing in my room Jade?" he demanded, grabbing a blanket and tossing it at her. "I'm not playing this game with you no more! Xanae left, you gotta get the fuck out!"

Jade didn't move to cover herself. Instead, she laughed and rolled onto her stomach, never taking her eyes off him.

"Relax Khi. She probably just needed some air. You must be used to her running when things get too real, I know it must be hard chasing after a girl when you have a woman standing right in front of you." She giggled, enjoying the game she was playing with his life.

"Jade, this ain't a joke. What did you do?" Khi demanded.

His judgment had been a prisoner of Jade's artistry, her uncanny talent for mesmerizing, for weaving seduction into every glance, every touch, until reason dissolved like smoke in the heat of her allure. Now he knew better, he realized something wasn't right last night. Xanae wasn't herself, she was drunk, maybe worse. The way she moved like a puppet on trembling strings, told him that whatever happened between her and Jade wasn't something she willingly chose. It wasn't something she was conscious enough to fight.

Now he had to face the aftermath. The trail of heartbreak and questions she left behind. Her engagement ring, abandoned like a broken promise, her cell phone discarded, a final severing of the life they had built together. Worst of all, she took their son, his son, without so much as a goodbye. It wasn't just a disappearance. It was a message, an unspoken cry, making Khi realize that there was nothing he could do to fix it this time.

Jade's smile didn't fade, her eyes revealed that she was unbothered.

"I don't know where she is. Maybe she ran because she can't handle being your woman. You ever think of that? She knew exactly what was going on last night, just like you did. So don't come at me like this is my fault."

Something inside Khi snapped. In a blur, he was on top of Jade, his hands wrapping around her throat as he pinned her against the mattress.

"Bitch, you think I'm playing with you?" he hissed. "This is my life you messing with!"

Jade didn't flinch.

"Did you forget?" she said, her voice barely audible as his grip tightened. "I'm carrying your daughter Khi. Whether you like it or not, I'm part of your life now."

Khi loosened his grip, pulling back as soon as he realized what he had done. Jade sat up slowly, then leaned forward, and pressed her breast against his back, gently massaging his shoulders.

"You're special Khi," she purred. "You need a woman who can handle being with a man like you. She's weak. Always running, but me? I've been here, even when it wasn't easy. Let me make it up to you." Jade encouraged.

The lies rolled off her tongue like venom, each word searing her lips with their burn. He wasn't special. He wasn't even worthy. The time they had shared had once been beautiful, an escape from the prison of her loneliness, a respite from the suffocating grip of her grief. In those moments, she had allowed herself to believe, to foolishly hope that he could be more, that he could be the man she had imagined in the corners of her mind. But then the truth came unexpectedly, tearing through the fragile illusion she had built. He was the enemy.

It wasn't just disappointment; it was devastation. The man she thought he could be was a mirage, a cruel trick of the light, and when she saw him for who he truly was, her entire world collapsed. The cracks in her heart that had been spawned from her husband's demise had spread wide, but they didn't bleed, they hardened, solidified, leaving behind something cold. Now, the lies she told weren't just a shield, they were the weapon she would use to ensure Khi felt the same destruction he had unknowingly caused in her.

Khi didn't respond. He didn't trust her, but there was something about the way she spoke, the way she knew just what to say to make him question everything.

"Come on, I've got something special planned for us tomorrow night, after that, if you really want me to go back to Miami, I will. No questions asked. I'll only reach out if it's about our daughter." She said, holding up her right hand.

Khi turned slightly, slanting his eyes at her. "Something special like what?" He asked.

"It's a surprise," Jade said, with a playful smile. "Trust me, you'll love it. Just be home by seven."

Khi exhaled deeply, his mind was cluttered with so many emotions he didn't know how to feel. He was starting to think that Jade was right, maybe Xanae wasn't the woman he needed by his side. She knew his story, she knew that being abandoned was his worst fear. A fear that had been carved into his soul by his Traumatic childhood, yet she had walked out on him more times than he could count, leaving him to pick up the shattered pieces of his trust every single time. He was out there grinding, risking everything to secure a future where they would never have to struggle again. But instead of standing beside him, Xanae was always pushing him to leave the game, to change in ways he wasn't ready for. Still, despite all of it, he hadn't given up on her.

Jade, on the other hand, was different. She knew all the right things to say to make him feel invincible. She was beautiful in a way that turned heads and strong in a way that demanded respect.. But no matter how flawless Jade seemed, she wasn't Xanae. She never could be. As much as Xanae frustrated him, as much as she tested his limits, she was the only one who made him dream of a life beyond survival. And that was a feeling Jade could never touch.

"I'll see what I can do," Khi replied, as he stood and walked toward the door without another look at her.

Jade smiled as the door clicked shut behind Khi. She knew the way his heartbeat for Xanae, the way her name turned soft in his mouth like it was made of silk. But none of that mattered to her now. Shadows danced across the room, as if they were reflecting the dark, simmering truth hidden in her mind. Tomorrow night the curtain would lift, and the first act of her carefully scripted plan would unfold. She caught a glimpse of herself in the mirror, the fury in her silver eyes was sharper than any blade. It was an unforgiving, dreadful promise of what was to come. Soon, Khi wouldn't just lose Xanae, he would lose everything, and she would finally be able to breathe again after holding in the pain, the resentment, the truth that had been delivered to her unexpectedly. A truth that had crippled her.

Chapter 19

Xanae's palms were damp with sweat as she moved them back and forth along the steering wheel. Each breath she took felt shallow, as though the air itself was resisting her lungs.

"You're here now," she whispered. Just go inside... Just... go... inside." She repeated.

She couldn't will herself to move, no matter how hard she tried. She stared at the house in front of her, it still looked exactly the same. Memories of past laughter and love came flooding back, making her miss everything she had lost. She exhaled and finally forced herself to get out of the car.

KJ was fast asleep in his car seat, his tiny chest rising and falling in the tranquil rhythm of a child untouched by the world around him. Xanae lifted him carefully, cradling him against her, praying that his small, steady heartbeat might calm her own.

The chipped paint on the railing, rocking chairs, and the sound of the loose boards on the porch, were all so familiar, as though the house had been waiting for her to return.

She paused at the door, her courage decreasing by the second, as heartbreaking memories pressed against her like an invisible hand. Summoning every ounce of strength she could muster; she knocked with three firm thuds that landed against the wooden frame. The sound seemed louder than it should have, bouncing back like a challenge to her own fear. She held her breath, waiting.

The door flew open, startling her. “Nae! Nae, baby, is that you?” Mama P shouted with disbelief and joy, as she stared at Xanae with tears in her eyes.

Relief surged through Xanae’s body, and she finally released a breath she didn’t realize she had been holding. Mama P’s face was so warm and loving, like a beacon piercing through the fog of guilt and shame that had consumed Xanae for years.

“Oh my God, it’s cold out here. Bring that baby on in,” Mama P said, pulling Xanae and KJ inside, her voice was full of sincerity and urgency.

The moment Xanae stepped through the threshold, the house seemed to embrace her. The rich scents of cinnamon and Fabuloso wrapped around her, pulling her into the past. Nothing had changed. The worn brown leather sofa still sat in the living room with the crocheted afghan draped over its armrest like a relic of comfort. As Mama P bustled off with KJ, carrying him toward the back room, Xanae stood rooted to the spot, her eyes drawn to the fireplace mantel. She focused on a picture of her and KoKo at sixteen, arms wrapped around each other, grinning like they had the whole world ahead of them. Her fingers trembled as she reached for it, the cool glass of the frame pressing into her palm offered a fragile comfort just before the floodgates broke, unleashing the downpour she had held back for far too long.

The tears came hard and fast, causing her body to shake from the force of her sobs. She clutched the frame to her chest as though it could heal her internal wounds, but it couldn't. Years of guilt and grief spilled out, raw and uncontrollable.

"It's okay baby. It's okay," Mama P said, her voice was soft and steady, as she appeared beside Xanae, gently placing a hand on her back. She guided her to the sofa, sitting with her like she had so many times before.

"Mama P, I'm so sorry. I'm so, so sorry." Xanae cried, her words tumbling out between gasps for air. She rocked back and forth, as heavy tears fell, and her pain spilled out of her.

"I wanted to come see you, I wanted to tell you everything, but I... I didn't know how."

Mama P cupped Xanae's face with both hands, her deep brown eyes filled with love and heartbreak.

"Shhhhh. It's okay. I'm just happy you're here now. We thought you were dead baby. What took you so long to come home?" She asked, trying to raise Xanae's head so that their eyes could meet.

Xanae's shoulders heaved as she inhaled deeply, desperate to steady herself.

"I was scared," she whispered. "I thought everyone blamed me… I thought everyone hated me. And so much happened, everything happened so fast." She explained.

Mama P shook her head, a single tear tracing the curve of her cheek. "We never blamed you Nae. Never. All these years, all we've wanted is to know what really happened to KoKo and to you."

Xanae wiped her damp face and finally forced herself to meet Mama P's gaze.

Mama P had been her savior, her second mother after losing her own. Her real name was Patricia, but Xanae had called her Mama P for as long as she could remember, and now the shame of failing her threatened to crush her. She knew she owed her the truth.

"I...I don't even know where to start," Xanae stammered.

Mama P leaned closer and gripped Xanae's hand tightly. "Start at the beginning Nae. Tell me everything. No matter how hard it is, I want to know."

Xanae closed her eyes and drew in a shuddering breath. Slowly, she began to peel back the layers of secrets and pain, recounting every moment, every choice, every detail that led to KoKo's death and the shattered years that followed. As the story unfolded, Mama P sobbed, the anguish that had haunted her for two long years finally coming out. When Xanae finished, silence enveloped the room.

Mama P pulled Xanae into her arms, their tears mingling in the space between them. "I never blamed you, Xanae," she whispered fiercely. "I'm glad you're home.

Baby, whatever you're holding on to, you have to let it go. Forgive yourself. KoKo would want that. And Rah will be so happy when he hears you're back. I know he'll come home now." Mama P said with a relieved smile.

The sound of Rah's name sent a vibration through Xanae's chest. Memories surged forward like a flood: Rah's laughter, his touch, the way his eyes held promises she thought would last forever. He had been her first love, her first kiss, her first everything. Before Khi, she hadn't thought it was possible to love anyone the way she loved Rah. But Rah had forced her to move on, leaving her with no choice.

Her mind spiraled back to the day everything changed. Rah had been sentenced to ten years for attempted murder, and she had promised to wait for him. She answered every call, sent letters weekly, and visited him without fail. Until one day she showed up for their visit and the correctional officer told her that her name had been permanently removed from the visitation list.

She waited for weeks to hear from him, her heart breaking a little more each day, finally a letter arrived.

Baby Girl,

I know you're confused, but please hear me out. I'm not doing this to hurt you, I'm doing it because I love you more than anything in this world. You are a Queen, and you deserve so much more than I can give you behind these walls. I can't ask you to put your life on hold for me, even though I know you would because you're just that solid. I will never love another woman the way I love you Xanae. I would die for you, but I need you to live for me. Don't wait for my calls, don't write, and don't try to come see me. JUST LIVE.

Forever & Ever.

Love Rah.

Mama P's voice broke through the haze of Xanae's memories.

"He normally calls me every week and sends money every month, always more than I need. I told him to stop, but you know that boy doesn't listen. I haven't heard from him this week." She said sadly.

Xanae blinked, trying to process what Mama P was telling her. "He sends you money from prison. How?" She asked.

"Prison? Baby, you don't know, do you? Rah was released over a year ago. He couldn't stay here after losing you and KoKo. He said it was too much for him. He left North Carolina and I haven't seen him since. Even though I wish he would come back, I understand." Mama P explained.

The words crashed into Xanae, landed in the pit of her stomach and burst through her heart. Rah was *home*. He had been free for over a year. Everything she thought she knew shattered in an instant. The thought of facing him, of explaining her engagement and her baby, made her sick to her stomach.

"Mama P, that drive was long and I'm not feeling well. Can I lay down for a little bit?" Xanae asked.

Mama P gave her a knowing look but didn't press. "Of course baby. This is still your home. Rest as long as you need to."

Xanae stared at the four walls in the room she once shared with KoKo, the memories swirled around her. Every corner of the space seemed to echo with their laughter, and secrets. She curled up beside KJ, biting her lip to keep the tears at bay. *Tomorrow.* She thought..... Tomorrow, she would face what she had been avoiding for years.

The next morning, the smell of blueberry pancakes drifted into the room. For the first time in a long time, Xanae had slept through the night. She woke up feeling lighter.

In the kitchen, she found Mama P feeding KJ tiny bites of pancakes, both of them smiling as bright as the morning sun. "Mama P, are you sure he can eat that, he's only 5 months" Xanae teased, sliding into a seat.

"Chile, I raised two kids- three if you count ya self. This baby wants real food!" Mama P chuckled.

For a second everything felt normal. Safe. Xanae made herself at home and piled 3 pancakes, bacon and eggs on her plate. She finally had an appetite after days of being unable to eat, and Mama P's cooking was the perfect first meal. She at every crumb and smiled in satisfaction as she moved to do the dishes.

"Don't worry about that baby, I'll do them. Mama P said with a warm smile.

"No, no Mama P, you've done enough. The least I can do is the dishes" Xanae insisted

When she finished the last dish, she knew it was time. "Mama P, can you watch KJ? There's something I need to do; I've put it off for way too long." Xanae said, her voice carrying a quiet resolve.

Mama P studied her for a long moment, before she gave a slow nod.

"Take all the time you need baby. I'll write down the address for you."

She didn't ask questions; she didn't need to. She knew that some battles had to be fought alone.

Xanae took the paper, gripping it tightly as if it were a lifeline. Today, she wasn't running. No more hiding, no more second-guessing. Today, she was staring the past dead in the face, ready to rip the truth wide open and carve a path back to the woman she used to be, the woman she was before the lies, before the betrayal, before Khi. She was done surviving. It was time to take her power back.

KJ giggled, his tiny hands flailing with joy, as Mama P bounced him on her thigh. His laughter was soothing, a reminder that even in the middle of treachery, life still had room to bloom.

■■

Xanae sat in her truck, staring out at the gray expanse of the cemetery, her fingers drumming an anxious rhythm on the steering wheel. For nearly an hour, she had been lost in memories, replaying every decision, every moment she wished she could rewrite. Her mind wrestled with the impossible ways to change a past that had already carved its scars deep into her soul. Her heart pounded against her ribs as she whispered words of courage to herself, hollow promises to face the monster of her guilt. But beneath it all, she was terrified.

Finally, with a sharp inhale, she gripped the door handle and pushed it open, the cold air rushing in to meet her. Her boots crunched against the frost-bitten ground as she moved. She could see her breath in the frigid air as she murmured softly to herself.

Sadness swept over her as she made her way through the endless rows of headstones, each one a monument to a life left behind. When her eyes landed on KoKo's name, she stopped in her tracks. The sight hit her like a blow to the head, and her knees buckled as she collapsed into the wet grass. The icy chill soaked through her jeans, but she didn't care.

The tears came in an unrelenting wave, blurring her vision as she reached out to touch the cold stone.

"KoKo..." she choked, her voice breaking. "I'm so sorry. I'm so, so sorry." The words tumbled out, raw and unfiltered, as if saying them aloud could somehow undo the pain. She talked to KoKo as if she were sitting right beside her, pouring out everything that had happened in the past two years. She told her about the heartbreak, the mistakes, the moments she had been too afraid to speak of to anyone else. She didn't hold back, didn't leave anything unsaid.

As the minutes turned to hours, her tears transitioned to laughter as she shared stories from their childhood, moments only the two of them had understood.

"I love you, I hope you can forgive me." she whispered.

At that moment, the air shifted around her. The biting cold seemed to soften, and the dreary clouds parted as sunlight spilled across the cemetery like a silent blessing. Xanae tilted her face upward, the warmth of the sun on her skin felt like a sign, as though KoKo was reaching down to her, wrapping her in love and reassurance. In her heart, she knew that KoKo was in heaven, and now she also knew that she didn't blame her.

"Koko, I love you," Xanae said softly, her tears now carrying something closer to peace. "You are my sister, and I will *never* forget you. I promise to visit as much as I can.

Save a spot up there for me, okay?" She kissed her fingers and pressed them to the headstone, her heart lighter than it had been in years.

When she made it back to her truck, she let out a deep breath. Making peace with KoKo had sparked something deep within her, a hunger for closure that she had avoided for far too long. The thought of Khi bothered her. The way she had walked away without truly saying goodbye, leaving loose ends that refused to be tied. She knew him well enough to know that he would never stop looking for her.

As she gazed into her reflection in the rearview mirror, her eyes carried a new light. She couldn't find true peace until she confronted the past, not just KoKo, but everything she had been running from. She knew she had to go back to Georgia. She wasn't going back to reopen wounds; she was going back to close them the right way.

With another deep breath, she started the engine, ready to begin the hardest but most necessary part of her journey: finding herself again.

Chapter 20

Trinity paced the the dingy hotel room, as she tried to figure out her next move. The room smelled faintly of mildew, its dirty carpet littered with unidentifiable stains. The lumpy mattress sagged in the middle, and the air was so cold she could see her breath fogging before her. But none of that mattered. No one would think to look for her in a place like this, and for now, that was enough.

She ran her fingers through her unkempt hair, her nails digging into her scalp as she talked to herself. Killing Reese had been reckless. She knew that. But she couldn't let him go through with the hit on Khi, it could have been anyone else, but not Khi. Despite everything, she still clung to the impossible fantasy that she could warn him, make him see her differently, and somehow salvage what was left of their connection.

If I could just get close to him... just close enough. I could make him see how much I care. And Xanae....I'll handle her. Khi doesn't even need to know. She thought, her mind racing.

But no matter how she spun it, nothing seemed to work. Every plan unraveled under the weight of reality. Her frustration boiled over, as she slammed her fist against the flimsy bedside table. She closed her eyes, trying to steady herself. Letting go of Khi wasn't an option, not for her. Not after everything.

For as long as she could remember, she had fantasized about being a part of his life, about being his little sister, about sharing in the unshakable love and security he gave Harmony. But that dream had never been hers to claim. Now that she had experienced him, Khi and KJ were her family in her own twisted mind, and she wasn't ready to give that up.

The sharp knock at the door snapped her out of her thoughts, and her heart leapt into her throat. She froze mid-step, her body stiff with fear. *No one should know I'm here.* She thought, her pulse thundering in her ears.

"Ma'am? Ma'am, it's housekeeping," a muffled voice called from the other side of the door. "The heat is out in the building, so the front office sent us to bring some extra blankets." The housekeeper uttered.

Trinity exhaled shakily, relief washing over her after hearing the woman's voice. She hurried to the door, her body shivering from the cold that had seeped into her bones. When she opened it, she smiled weakly at the small Hispanic lady holding a bundle of blankets.

But before she could say a word, the blankets fell to the ground, and Trinity found herself staring down the barrel of a .45 pistol.

Her stomach dropped. She watched in stunned silence as the housekeeper scurried away, clutching a hundred-dollar bill Reese had slipped her. He stepped into the room, locking the door behind him with a sickening *click.*

"Bet I'm the last person you expected to see," Reese said with a sneer, his voice was like gravel as he motioned for her to sit. His gun traced slow, mocking circles in the air, daring her to defy him.

"So this was your master plan? Take what's mine, try to take me out, and dip off to some crusty-ass motel like I wouldn't track you down? Reese growled. This?" Reese gestured around the shabby room with the gun. "This is where you thought it would all end? I thought you were smarter than that Trinity. Smarter than to play me like I'm one of these street niggas that's easy to finesse." His voice dropped lower, more dangerous, as he leaned closer. "But nah... tonight, you gone learn what it means to really cross me."

Trinity stumbled back into a chair; her legs barely able to hold her. She couldn't look away from the gun, its dark barrel was like a pit she was about to fall into. She couldn't believe Reese had survived the poisonous dinner;

she cursed herself for not making sure he was dead before she made her escape.

"Reese, I-"

"Save it," Reese interrupted, with an evil smirk.

He stepped closer, trailing the tip of the gunalong her jawline, causing the cold steel to send chills down her spine.

"You tried to kill me, and you failed. Now you gotta deal with the consequences. And I promise, you're gonna wish I *was* dead by the time I'm through with you." Reese spat.

Trinity's heart raced as he grabbed a fistful of her hair, yanking her head back. She winced, but she didn't cry out. She wouldn't give him the satisfaction. "Reese, please, I didn't-"

"Shut up," he snapped.

"The details of the hit have changed, but only because I figured you already tried to warn him. Am I right?"

"I didn't, I swear, I came straight here." Trinity said as she tried to stop her heart from thudding in her chest.

Reese studied her, unable to tell if she was lying or not.

"Even if you did, it doesn't matter. I never leave a job unfinished. It's still happening, and you're gonna be the one to pull the trigger. MASK OFF." Reese said, his voice a sinister rumble.

Trinity's heart sank as the words exploded out of Reese.

"No," she whispered. "I can't. I won't." She cried, the tears blurred her vision, but she could still see the ice in Reese's eyes.

She shook her head frantically, but deep down, she knew there was no room for refusal. It was bad enough that she was a part of the hit, complicit in this nightmare. But *this*? The thought of staring Khi in the eyes, bare-faced, and pulling the trigger, watching the light leave the man who once meant everything to her, was unbearable.

Reese's grip on her hair tightened, forcing her to meet his eyes. "Oh, you will," he whispered. "Because if you don't, you are as dead as he is. It's really simple Tee, either Khi dies, or you both do."

A sob escaped her lips as the reality of her situation crashed over her. Reese wasn't bluffing. He was ruthless, and she knew from experience that there was no reasoning with him. Her mind screamed for a way out, but there wasn't one.

Trinity stared at the floor, her tears falling silently onto the dirty carpet. There was no escape, no redemption. Reese had stripped her of the last shred of control she thought she had. And now, she had to decide: Khi's life, or her own.

Xanae glanced at the new phone she purchased for what felt like the hundredth time. Nervous energy filled her as she checked how much longer it would be until her Uber driver arrived. She had made the decision to catch a flight back to Georgia instead of driving; the four-hour drive would have given her too much time to overthink, to doubt herself, to turn around and convince herself it wasn't worth it. The 45-minute flight with the hustle and bustle of the Airport, TSA line and dozens of passengers didn't allow for second-guessing. She needed to see Khi. She needed answers. She needed closure.

The soft chime of her phone pulled her from her spiraling thoughts. Her driver was finally outside. Tossing her bag over her shoulder, she made her way to the white Hyundai idling by the curb and slid into the back seat without hesitation. She sat quietly, inhaling the pine-scented air freshener and staring out the window as the car sped through the streets. Her mind was already focused on what she might say when she saw Khi. She prayed that her heart and his would accept it.

Twenty minutes later, the Uber driver pulled up to the house, the same house that used to be hers. The sight of it made her emotional. This was where she and Khi were supposed to build their life, where they had dreamed of a future together. Now it felt like a stranger's house.

Her eyes darted to the driveway. Khi's car wasn't there. Her heart sank and then rose again in a confusing mix of feelings she couldn't quite explain. Should she call him?

Let him know she was back? The thought flickered briefly, but she dismissed it. No, she needed his raw, unfiltered truth. She needed to hear his words without the shield of preparation. She didn't want him rehearsing an explanation or smoothing over the cracks of their broken relationship. And most importantly, he needed to hear her truth, the unvarnished version she had been holding inside for far too long.

She still had the keys to the house, and as she slid the familiar metal into the lock, her hands shook. Stepping inside, she was met with an eerie silence, the kind that made the air feel heavier. The scent of lavender lingered faintly, triggering memories that clung to the space. She closed the door softly behind her, disarmed the alarm, and stood there for a moment, letting everything settle in.

The house was immaculate, as if nothing had changed, yet everything was different. Each room she passed felt like walking through a museum of their life together. The furniture, the framed pictures, the tiny details they had chosen together, it all felt foreign now. When she reached the master bedroom her heart sank.

A red silk robe, lay draped across the bed. She realized that Jade was still there. A cold sweat broke out along Xanae's forehead as her heart hammered against her ribs. She had imagined Khi broken, devastated by her absence, unable to function without her. But this? This felt like betrayal layered on top of heartbreak. Not only had he stayed with Jade, but it looked like he was thriving, enjoying playing house in the space that used to be theirs.

Xanae's legs felt weak, and she started to get lightheaded. She stumbled back from the room, needing to put as much distance as possible between herself and the painful reminder of what Khi had moved on to. She made her way to one of the guest rooms they never used, the only space in the house untouched by memories of Khi and Jade. She collapsed onto the bed, her body trembling as tears fell against her will.

Lying there, staring up at the ceiling, she tried to steady herself. She hadn't come all this way to fall apart. She had come for answers, she wanted it all to be over. Whenever Khi decided to walk through that door, she would be ready. Ready to tell him exactly how she felt about everything, the lies, the heartbreak, and especially Jade. If this chapter of her life was going to end, she was going to make damn sure it ended on her terms.

Chapter 21

Jade looked at the clock, it was almost 6:45. She took a large sip from her wine glass and checked to make sure everything was perfect. Tonight was the night that she had been waiting on for so long. When she heard the back door open, she immediately ran over to greet Khi.

"You made it home before 7, thank you baby. She said kissing him as she handed him a glass of wine.

Khi tried his best to smile but the truth was he was miserable. Jade was cool, and she was carrying his child but he was broken over Xanae. He needed to see her, hold her, talk to her and his son, but he had no idea where she was, and it was slowly killing him inside.

"Ima go change" Khi replied before heading upstairs.

Jade could feel the tension between them, but she didn't care. Khi was a grown ass man and he had to live with the decisions that he had made. She began preparing their plates, the aroma of the snapper and curried potatoes filled the room. Jade placed Khi's plate on the table just as he came back in the kitchen and took a seat.

Khi knew that she was trying, and that the scenario wasn't ideal for her either. He stood and began walking towards Jade to give her a hug and thank her for the dinner when suddenly he heard the back door open. He instinctively reached for the kitchen drawer where he had a 9-millimeter hidden, but it wasn't there. Before he had a chance to make a move, two assailants entered.

"Where the fuck is my shit" Khi thought as he stared intently at the intruders. The gun was always there. He kept a piece in every room just in case something like this ever happened he could be prepared.

"You move, you die" Reese said as he walked towards Khi, gun in hand, while Trinity proceeded to grab Jade.

"Khi, what is going on, who are these people?" Jade cried as Trinity pointed the gun at her and escorted her out of the kitchen before Khi could respond.

"Who sent you?" Khi asked, as he waited for the man to make his next move.

"What makes you think I was sent? I'm here for the money nigga. Show me to the safe" Reese replied.

"The money? Money ain't no object. You tell me who sent you and I'll double whatever the offer is. Ain't no safe here, so it's either clue me in on who sent you, or you gonna leave empty handed my nigga" Khi retorted.

He was so angry that he had been caught slipping in his own home, he knew that he had enable the security system and locked the door when he came in. He wondered how the intruders had managed to get in so effortlessly. He didn't know how long the guns had been missing from their hiding places or when someone could have taken them, but it was clear that there was a snake in his camp.

His mind was so wrapped up in his business dealings with Cruz and Biggs and the issues he was having with Xanae, along with the problems with Jade he wasn't moving like he normally would.

"You ain't in control this time lil nigga. You don't have to show me the safe but trust me I will find it" Reese replied just before slapping Khi across the face with his gun and dragging him to the living room.

"Ahhh, you muthafucka, Ima kill you" Khi yelled as he fought against being taken into the other room.

Jade's sobs cut through the air. "Khi, what is this? What do they want?" she cried, her voice fractured with terror. Bound to a chair in the center of the room, she looked every bit the victim. Her eyes were wet with tears, and her hands were clenched into trembling fists, but the way she scanned the room, going from Reese, Trinity, and Khi, hinted that there was something else beneath the panic.

"It's ok Jade, Ima pay these niggas off. They looking for the safe," Khi said. His words were steady, but his jaw tensed as Reese shoved him into the chair beside her.

The restraints bit into his wrists as the second assailant worked silently. Trinity didn't want to speak, fearing Khi would know it was her. Khi's sharp eyes never left her. He clocked her movements, her stance, even the shaky hesitation in her fingers. Recognition sparked faintly in his mind, but he held it close, waiting for the right moment.

"Shut the fuck up!" Reese snapped, his voice ricocheting off the walls. "We can do this the easy way or the hard way. Your choice." He began to prowl around the room, flipping furniture, yanking drawers open, and scattering papers in a show of destruction.

"You wasting your time, do you think I'm dumb enough to keep my money here?" Khi said as he shifted his focus to Reese, making sure his peripheral vision traced Trinity's every step. He recognized her, her build, her eyes, her mannerisms. He noticed the flicker of vulnerability. She didn't want to be here. Not like this.

Reese smirked, tossing a framed photo to the floor where it shattered. "Oh, I'm wasting my time huh? Well it looks like you need to PAY for wasting my time!" He barked, turning to Trinity.

"Shoot this nigga right between the eyes."

Trinity's hands shook slightly, the cold metal of the gun felt like jello. She could barely move, as her finger hovered, uncertain, over the trigger. Suddenly Khi's voice cut through her, each word carefully chosen, sharp as a surgeon's scalpel.

"Do you remember your fifth birthday?" Khi began, each word a careful thread in the delicate tapestry of a lie. His tone softened, as if cradling her in the memory he was crafting just for her.

"We went to see the ponies and we walked around the park eating our Strawberry ice cream cones with sprinkles. Remember it was your favorite? You always begged for it." Khi said with a forced smile.

Trinity slowly nodded. Khi could see the change in body language. She was reliving a past that wasn't hers, recounting memories and events that she longed for as a little girl.

The words felt jagged in his throat, each syllable scraping against the truth that was buried long ago. His voice was filled with emotion, curling around his words like smoke, designed to pull her in.

"You were so happy; we stayed until the stars came out. You couldn't even keep your eyes open anymore." He continued the façade, but in his mind the truth roared back with cruel clarity, slicing through the fog of his performance. Chocolate. Harmony's favorite ice cream had always been chocolate, never strawberry. She couldn't have eaten strawberries even if she wanted to, she was allergic. The small detail had revealed the truth. A truth that felt like a knife in his chest, a fresh wound tearing open as he acknowledged what he had been trying so desperately to avoid. Trinity wasn't Harmony. Harmony was gone. Forever. Xanae had been right all along.

His heart hurt so badly, he felt as though he might crumble under the pain, but he couldn't, he wouldn't. He swallowed hard, his Adam's apple bobbing as he forced the tears back, his expression remained composed, even as he shattered piece by piece on the inside.

He met Trinity's eyes, her trembling hand still gripping the gun, and pushed the words out, each one tasting like ash. "Trinity, I'm your brother. KJ is your nephew. We love you."

The lie scorched him on its way out, the burn searing his soul, but he didn't flinch. He couldn't. His life dangled on a thread as thin as the one holding her sanity together. He waited, watching her, praying that she would take the bait, praying she would do something, anything, to save him.

Khi's words pressed down on her, dismantling the fragile reality she had built brick by brick in her fractured mind. Her mask slipped, first figuratively, then literally, as she pulled it away, revealing her face. Her wide eyes, shimmered with tears as she stared at him.

Khi felt the importance of that moment, her insanity was both a gift and a curse. He could see it in her expression: the war between what her heart clung to and what her mind couldn't reconcile.

Jade watched the scene unfold; confusion ran across her face as she tried to decipher the odd exchange. The silence stretched heavy for a moment, until she shattered it with a sudden command.

"Enough," she snapped, her tone slicing through the air like a whip. Her voice was firm now, carrying an authority that left no room for argument.

"Untie me." The words were directed squarely at Reese, as she stared at him with unflinching intensity.

Reese hesitated- he never hesitated. He wanted to be sure he heard her clearly before he made any moves.

"Untie you?" he repeated, as if he couldn't quite process the request. He regretted going forward with this job. He had never taken a hit so tangled, so volatile. From the start, something felt off, but the payout that dangled in front of him had been too tempting to ignore. Reese had nothing left to lose, nothing but one fragile tether to a person he loved, someone he convinced himself would survive just fine without him. He filled that void with recklessness, throwing himself into dangerous jobs, chasing the rush of feeling something, anything beyond the dull ache of his regrets.

That recklessness had led him here. Led him to Trinity. At first, she had intrigued him. There was fire in her, a raw, chaotic energy that mirrored his own buried turmoil. She was cold, calculating, broken in ways that felt familiar, a dark reflection of himself. For a short time, she had felt like a sanctuary, someone who didn't expect him to be whole or good. But fascination had soured into frustration, and Trinity had become, a liability and clearly an adversary.

As he stood there now, Jade's demand echoing in the air, Reese felt the aftermath of his choices. The excuses he had fed himself, the habits he had let slip, the ways he had allowed bitterness and pain to shape his actions all stared back at him in the mirror of this moment. For the first time in a long time, he realized with a pang of shame that he didn't like the man he'd become.

"Now!" Jade snapped, pulling Reese back to the present. Khi's heartbeat quickened as Reese crossed the room, his hands moving swiftly to remove the restraints from Jade. Every step Reese took felt surreal, like a nightmare unfolding in slow motion.

"Jade?!" Khi's voice cracked, confusion and disbelief bleeding into his tone. "You did this? You set me up? Why? You're carrying my daughter, why would you do this?" His words came out uneven and his heart pounded in his chest as his mind raced to piece together a puzzle that felt impossible to solve.

Jade scoffed, her laugh bitter and hollow. "Spare me the bullshit Khi, the baby probably isn't even yours." Jade spat. She spoke in a tone that he had never heard from her before. Each word was filled with animosity.

The room seemed to shrink around Khi as her words sank in, leaving him stunned and motionless. For the first time, he saw her genuine hate for him. It was raw and unfiltered, brimming in her grey eyes. Those eyes, once warm and inviting, now burned cold as ice. Every glance she threw his way felt like a dagger aimed at his heart. How had he been so blind? He had destroyed his life with Xanae for

Jade's lies. A child he thought was his wasn't, and all this time he had been a pawn in her game. But why? What had he done to her that could justify this level of malice? It couldn't just be about Xanae.

Reese and Trinity stood off to the side, confused as they watched the exchange unfold. Reese, shifted on his feet, but kept his silence. He hadn't told Trinity that Jade was the client who had ordered the hit on Khi, she couldn't be trusted, the less Trinity knew, the better.

Jade took a step forward, her entire body quivering as if her fury could no longer be contained.

"You want to know why, Khi?" she whispered, trying to conceal her voice breaking under the weight of her anguish. "You're responsible for taking away the only thing in this world that ever mattered to me." She paused, her chest heaving as memories surged to the surface.

"All of this started because of you. Rock told me everything! You were the one that killed my husband. You fucking evil bastard! You had the audacity to let me get close to you, to pretend like I'm the one that ruined YOUR life! Do you have any idea what losing him did to me, what you took from me?" She cried.

He was the love of my life. My everything." Her words faltered as her mind replayed the memories of West's laugh, the way his arms felt around her, the plans they had made for a future that would never come.

"He's gone. Gone because of you, and the worst part is, for the rest of my life I might be stuck with a reminder of the person that caused me the worst pain I've ever known."

How could something so innocent grow from something so dirty? So broken? She didn't know if she could love it. Didn't even know if she wanted to try.

Khi stood paralyzed, every word hitting him like a tidal wave, each revelation pulling him deeper into a fire that he never saw coming. Rock had to be playing chess, because somehow, he had maneuvered his way into Xanae's world, slipping past walls Khi himself had not been allowed to breach.

Then there was Jade, convinced beyond doubt that he had killed a man he had never even laid eyes on. It all made sense now. The missing guns. That surprise "gift" at a party that was supposed to be invite-only. Jade's obsession with tearing him down. Rock had his fingerprints on every inch of it, he had been orchestrating Khi's downfall from the shadows.

Khi never thought robbing Dame would set off a chain reaction like this, a single reckless decision led to so much destruction. Now he was left drowning in the wreckage of his own choices.

"Pull the fucking trigger!" Reese barked. His patience was razor-thin, his frustration mounting. This hit was spiraling, becoming too personal, too messy. Normally, his jobs were surgical, clean and efficient. In and out. But this? This was chaotic. He could have ended it himself, but he wanted Trinity to pull the trigger. She had crossed him and killing her outright was too easy. She needed to to prove herself worthy of keeping her life after the stunt she had pulled.

Trinity hesitated. Her chest rose and fell as she fought against herself, waiting for that familiar, burning exhilaration, she always felt before a kill. The flame refused to ignite. Her hands shook as she slowly pointed the gun towards Khi.

"I… I…" She stumbled over the words, struggling to summon the cold detachment she usually thrived on.

"I CAN'T!" she screamed, spinning the gun toward Reese.

"I CAN."

Xanae emerged from the shadows, her movements swift, her eyes locked on Trinity. Without hesitation, she raised the gun in her hands and fired. The shots echoed like thunder, shattering the room's fragile silence. One, two, three... she didn't stop until her gun clicked empty. And even then, she pulled the trigger four more times.

She lowered the gun slowly, her expression emotionless as she stepped closer. Trinity lay on the floor, gasping in a pool of blood that was quickly turning the tile floors a crimson red. Xanae stared down at her, unmoved by her struggles. Her thoughts drifted to KoKo, but she didn't take her eyes off Trinity's until she was sure she had taken her last breath.

This was supposed to be the moment she found peace, the end of the nightmare she had been living. But as she watched the light fade from Trinity's eyes, there was no relief, no elation. Only sorrow and regret, filled her soul. The air in the room felt thick with unresolved energy, choking her.

A voice broke the silence, smooth and mocking.

"Well, well, well. Look who decided to join the party."

Jade stepped forward, her heels clicking against the blood-slick floor as she crouched by Trinity's lifeless body. She reached out, plucking the gun from her limp hands with a smirk. "Your timing couldn't have been better Xanae." Her tone was almost playful, but her eyes gleamed with malice.

Xanae cringed as soon as she heard Jade's voice. The sound was like nails on a chalkboard, grating against every nerve in her body. She hated Jade with a fiery passion, and as she glanced around the room, the heavy, suffocating negativity confirmed what she already knew: Jade was the source.

"Why is this bitch still here?" Xanae spat, her voice sharp as she started toward Khi.

"Nope! Don't fucking move!" Jade said with fury, as she leveled the gun at Xanae.

"She don't have shit to do with this! Let her go, and me and you can settle whatever we need to, Jade Please. Just let her go." Khi yelled.

Jade's face twisted into a sinister grin, the only thing she could think about was vindication.

"She does now. You took the love of my life away from me Khi. So, before I kill you, you're going to watch me take yours away from you."

Her hand tightened on the gun, and she raised it, pointing directly at Xanae's head.

"WAIT! KILL ME!" Khi's voice was raw, breaking under the strain of his emotions. "Shoot me, but let her go! He begged as he locked eyes with Jade, his pride was gone, replaced with sheer desperation. Khi was a man who didn't beg, but for Xanae, he would do anything. He knew the depths of Jade's hatred for Xanae, but he also knew that her hatred for him burned even hotter.

FA! FA! FA! FA!

"NOOOO!" Khi screamed, his voice filled with anguish as the gunshots rang out. His heart plummeted to the pit of his stomach, time seemed to stop, and his lungs felt heavy. Rage and despair surged through him as he thrashed against his restraints.

Then, a flicker of movement caught his eye. Xanae appeared behind him, her hands quickly untying the knots that bound him. Relief washed over him in an instant when he realized it wasn't Xanae who had fallen, it was Jade, crumpled on the floor, bleeding and gasping for air.

Xanae worked as fast as she could, moving rapidly as she glanced over her shoulder, half-expecting the other masked figure to stop her. Trinity's partner had been eerily silent throughout the chaos, but the shots fired had caused the room to blur into confusion. She didn't know why the masked man had saved her, but she wasn't about to question it.

"Xanae… Nae?" The voice stopped her cold.

The sound of her name hit her like a bolt of lightning. She turned slowly, standing there, mask now removed, was a face she hadn't seen in years, one she never thought she would see again.

"Rah?" Her voice was barely audible, shaken with disbelief. The room tilted as she tried to process what was happening. It was him. It was really him, standing there in the flesh, staring at her with those same eyes that had once held her entire world. Time seemed to collapse, years vanishing in an instant. He was different now. He was stronger, more defined. The boy she once knew was gone, replaced by a man whose presence commanded the room.

Her heart hammered in her chest, her thoughts racing. "How is he here? How did he find me?" she wondered, unable to move. She couldn't think, couldn't even feel anything past his energy.

Rah stared at her, the intensity in his eyes piercing through her. The connection between them was undeniable, like an unspoken force binding their souls together again.

"Nae?" Khi's voice broke through the trance, dragging her back to the present. She blinked, her lungs finally releasing the breath she had been holding.

"What's going on Xanae? You know him?" Khi asked in confusion.

"I... I..." Xanae stammered, unable to tear her eyes away from Rah. The words failed her as memories of love, of loss, and a bond too deep to explain surged to the surface. She couldn't go into details with Khi, not now, not like this. What she and Rah once shared was too profound, too layered. Their hearts had once beaten to the same rhythm, and even now, with everything between them, the fire burned just as brightly.

Rah stood tall; his broad shoulders squared as he stared at Khi silently. His presence alone spoke volumes; a quiet authority radiated from him like an unshakable force. Finally, he broke the silence.

"I'm her past, you're her present. She can decide her future." Rah said.

Without another word he reached into his pocket and pulled out a burner phone and handed it to Xanae. His fingers touched hers, causing the world to stand still for a second.

"I'm sorry Baby Girl. This shit wasn't supposed to go down like this. When this phone rings, make sure you answer it."

His words stayed in the air, heavy with meaning, as he backed away. Xanae's heart throbbed as she watched him disappear through the back door, leaving a trail of questions and unresolved feelings in his wake.

Chapter 22

Two days had crawled by since the nightmare with Trinity had ended, and the waiting game had begun. The brief relief Rah had provided had long since faded, leaving Xanae in a familiar state of unease. Anxiety clung to her like a second skin as she sat, nervously turning the phone Rah had given her over in her hands. She stared at it, willing it to ring. She just wanted to hear his voice, to know what he was feeling, where he was hiding, how he had been all these years. She needed answers.

Rah's sudden reappearance had reignited a flame she thought had long burned out. The memories of their encounter were vivid and consuming, crowding out everything else. Besides KJ, Rah was all she could think about. She missed her son desperately but knew she couldn't bring him back to Georgia. Mama P had promised to keep him safe and loved for as long as she needed, and for now, that had to be enough.

Still, she dreamed of Rah calling and them taking that drive together to see Mama P, but the phone stayed silent.

Her mind raced with insecurities and fears. ***Maybe he doesn't want to see me. Maybe he has a woman, kids… What if he's married?*** The thoughts hit her like a missile, and she shoved the phone into her pocket just as she heard Khi's footsteps approaching.

Khi had been relentless with his questions about Rah since their encounter, and each time Xanae had deflected, only offering vague responses. The truth was she loved Khi, but she also resented him. The last two years had been a whirlwind of trauma, and at the center of it all was Khi.

"Still waiting on that nigga to call, huh?" Khi's said bitterly as he entered the room, his hands tucked into his slacks.

"Khi, we grew up together. It's not what you think," Xanae said, standing straighter. "He's KoKo's brother. I can't just shut him out. I owe him an explanation."

She knew it was a half-truth. Rah was KoKo's brother, but that was only a fraction of their story.

"An explanation?" Khi's voice rose. "You don't owe him **shit**, Xanae! KoKo's death wasn't your fault baby. Why can't you see that?" He said, stepping closer, gently grabbing her shoulders and urging her to meet his eyes.

"I know it wasn't my fault Khi, but she was there because of me! If I never met you-" Xanae stopped herself, the words hanging in the air. She didn't want to say it, but the truth seared in her throat.

"If you never met me, what?" Khi pressed.

"If I never met you, she wouldn't have been there that night. This nightmare with Trinity would've never happened, and KoKo would still be alive!" Xanae cried.

Khi staggered back as if she had struck him.

"If you never met me?" he repeated, pounding his chest as tears filled his own eyes. Her words pierced him like a dagger, cutting straight to his soul. He had always known, deep down, that she might feel this way, but hearing it out loud was devastating. ***How could she ever truly love a man she blamed for her best friend's death?***

"This shit didn't start with me, Xanae!" Khi shouted! "It started with that nigga Dame, remember? Who's to say that crazy bitch wouldn't have tracked you down no matter where you were?"

He rarely raised his voice at Xanae, but the knot in his chest demanded release. Xanae was the only woman who had ever made him feel something real, the only one he had trusted enough to share his darkest truths. She was his light, the mother of his child, and now she was telling him she blamed him for all of it. She wasn't considering what the entire situation had done to him, how it had shattered him and sliced open old wounds he was still trying to heal from.

"I don't know that Khi, but I do know that Rah woke me up from the living hell I've been in for the past two years. He ***killed*** for me!" Xanae shot back

Khi's shoulders sagged, and he dropped his head, her words crushing him. All he had ever wanted was to give her the world, to marry her and build a life together. But no matter how hard he tried; it seemed like he only caused her pain.

"He killed for you, and I was willing to die for you Ma. So what you're telling me is, he loves you more than I do?" Khi questioned as he stared at her with pleading eyes.

Xanae's heart hurt at the sight of the man she loved breaking before her, but her emotions were a mess. She was torn between what was, and what could be, replaying Reese's words in her mind.

"I'm her past, you're her present, she can decide her future."

Khi took a deep breath and reached into his pocket, pulling out the engagement ring he had been holding onto. He gently lifted her left hand, his own trembling.

"Nae, I know this shit hasn't been easy. But you and KJ? You're the only things that I have left in this world that matter to me." He said as he fought back tears. "I'm getting out the game Ma, but it's gonna come at a cost."

"A cost?" Xanae whispered. "Khi, I have nothing else to lose except my life! What more do you want me to give up?"

"I don't want you to give up anything baby. I just need you to believe in me. Believe in ***us***. I have a plan. Our money won't be the same. I gotta give Cruz everything to pay my way out, but it doesn't matter. We can get out of here, lay low somewhere on an island, and just... just start over."

Xanae stared at him, disbelief and hope warring in her chest. "Are you serious? No more drugs? No dirty money? No more killing?"

"Nae, I'd give up the universe for you. If you're not in it, I don't need it. You and KJ are my life, and I promise we're gonna have our happily ever after. Just be patient with me Ma."

Her heart swelled at the thought of peace and freedom being within reach, but just as she was about to respond reality came crashing down.

"We have to move quick, though," Khi said, his tone shifting. "Sooner or later, Biggs is gonna start asking questions about Jade."

"Move quick? What does that mean?" Xanae asked, confusion clouding her face.

"That nigga ain't gonna let me breathe easy once he finds out what happened to her. Her blood is on my hands, and I gotta deal with him. But first, we gotta get outta here. Trust me Ma, I'm making the right decision. Khi pleaded.

Xanae's heart plummeted like a stone dropped into a dark well. "So now we're running? From the fucking Jamaican Mafia Khi?" Her voice quivered with fury. Khi's silence spoke louder than words. He wasn't asking; he was laying out her grim reality. A bitter choice hung between them, a life spent glancing over their shoulders, haunted by thoughts of the law busting down the door in the dead of night, or surrendering to the cold, merciless grip of the Jamaican mafia, with their family's lives dangling by a thread. The idea of both paths crushed her, each one a noose tightening around her future. Neither was a life she wanted to live.

Before he could respond, a familiar buzzing interrupted them. Xanae's heart leapt into her throat as she pulled Rah's phone from her pocket. It vibrated in her hand; she knew that the timing was the universe telling her to follow her heart.

She held her head high and turned to Khi.

"Me too." She said as she held up the phone, showing him the screen before quickly leaving the room to answer.

Khi wanted to run after her, to grab her and beg her not to leave, but he stayed rooted in place. He knew better. Words meant nothing now, and the look in her eyes told him she needed more than promises. She needed proof. If he didn't act, if he didn't move decisively, he was going to lose her. If he hadn't already.

He pulled out his phone and inhaled deeply as he prepared to make the call he had been dreading. The line between survival and a deadly war was razor-thin. If he didn't do something he knew Biggs would be coming soon, looking for Jade. Khi's mind raced as he thought through every detail of his plan, testing it for cracks. Noriega's crew had taken care of Jade's body, ensuring everything was clean and with a semblance of respect. But the aftermath of what had happened, and the innocent life Jade was carrying filled him with guilt. The thought of his seed, his flesh and blood, a piece of his own legacy being destroyed in a cyclone of betrayal and violence that was meant for him was too much to process. He shoved the thought away and whispered "***Hustle Now, Hurt Later***" just before Biggs answered the phone.

Chapter 23

Rah stared at the ceiling in his cabin, it had been months since he had been there. The soft creak of the walls as the wind pressed against them did nothing to settle his restless thoughts. It was Xanae, her face, her scent, her very essence, that consumed him. Her presence was intoxicating, a drug he had denied himself for too long. When she had vanished from his life, she took a part of him with her, leaving him hollow and hardened, relying only on survival and obligation to his mother to keep him moving forward. But now here she was, back in his orbit, and he wasn't sure if it was a blessing or a curse. His heart wanted to believe it was fate, that after all the broken pieces, they could fit back together again. He could still feel the warmth of her embrace, the silent promise it carried. The thought of opening up to her again scared him, but he craved it more than he feared it.

Suddenly his heart skipped a beat, snatching him from his thoughts and he knew she was close. A knock wasn't necessary; he felt her presence before she even touched the door. It was a pull, a connection that words could never explain. He was on his feet before he realized it, opening the door just as her knuckles touched the wood.

Their eyes met, then Rah stepped aside, allowing her in. As she passed, her arm brushed his chest, a brief touch that sent a ripple through his entire body. He took a deep breath to calm himself. No one could ever shake him like she did.

Xanae peered around the cabin. The rustic exterior hid the refined beauty inside. The polished wood floors gleamed under the soft light of the chandelier. A crackling fire danced in the background and candles filled the air with the sweet scent of cinnamon. Italian leather furniture framed the living space, and the large dining table was adorned with a fruit basket filled with bananas, mangoes, lemons, and apples.

Rah finally spoke "I'm glad you came Nae," he said, staring at her. He couldn't look away. Her beauty was different now, richer, more layered. Her curves were fuller, her face more defined, and her eyes were wells of untold stories and unhealed wounds.

Xanae exhaled, the tension in her shoulders melting away as relief washed over her. She had feared his rejection, unsure if he had forgiven her for the past. But those words and his tone told her what she needed to know. He didn't hate her.

As Rah stepped closer, the space between them evaporated, he tilted her chin up gently, his thumb grazing her jawline.

"I never blamed you Nae," he said, his voice filled with emotion. "Not for a second. If you could've taken that bullet for KoKo, I know you would have. That weight isn't yours to carry, it's mine. I should have been there to protect her, to protect you both. Trust me I will make damn sure the one responsible pays for what they did to her."

The fire in his words was undeniable, but so was the pain laced within them. She saw how deeply he had buried his grief. He still hadn't faced the memories waiting for him back home. The empty room, the swing in the backyard, the photos lining the walls. His vengeance was a shield, the only way he knew how to endure the devastation of losing his baby sister.

But he didn't know the truth, and as Xanae looked into his eyes, she realized that what she had to say would shatter him.

"Rah..." Her voice cracked, and tears spilled down her cheeks.

She hesitated, before forcing herself to say it. "The woman... Trinity. How did you know her?" Xanae asked.

Rah stiffened at the mention of her name. "She was... a work connection." The lie tasted bitter on his tongue, but he wasn't ready to open that door yet.

Xanae's breath shuddered. "Work? Rah, she's the one. She's the one who killed KoKo."

His world stopped as her words slammed into him.

"What? Trinity? She killed my sister?" He asked in disbelief.

"Yes, she was evil." Xanae nodded.

The rage came swiftly, erupting from a place buried so deep it had become a part of Rah. His mind spun as he tried to put the pieces of the puzzle together. He thought about the nights he had spent with the very woman who had ripped his heart apart. He fell to the floor, his body shaking as years of suppressed pain and anguish came pouring out in wrenching sobs. All the losses, all the guilt, all the love he had locked away, they escaped now.

Xanae was beside him in an instant, wrapping her arms tightly around him. She held him like she could keep him from shattering completely, her own tears mingling with his. No words passed between them, but their embrace spoke volumes. It was everything they both needed in the moment. Time stopped. The pain, the betrayal, the love, they shared it all. And for the first time in years, they felt something neither thought they would ever truly feel again.

Home.

Khi paced the floor, trying to figure out his next move. It had been two days since Xanae left and he still hadn't heard from her. He knew that she was with Rah and just thinking about what they could be doing was eating him alive. The situation with Biggs was at bay for now but Khi was no fool, eventually Biggs would seek answers for Jades disappearance, answers he had but couldn't provide. Khi was rethinking his rash decision to tell Biggs that Jade was missing and wished that he had made it seem like she was shot in a robbery gone wrong instead. Although Biggs would have still held him accountable, the consequences would have likely been less severe. The only reason Khi had opted to tell him that Jade was missing in the first place was to buy himself some time, time that he needed to plan his escape to paradise. It never occurred to him that Xanae would walk away and not agree to come with him. Leaving his woman and son wasn't an option, he had to figure out a way to kill his beef with Biggs, keep his money and get out of the game for good.

Ding Dong, Ding Dong...

"Who the fuck is that?" Khi thought as he walked over to his desk to look at the cameras.

He saw Detective Connelly holding a piece of paper in his hand along with two uniformed officers.

Khi stared at the cameras in confusion, wondering why Connelly would show up unannounced. His mother's case was closed months ago. His heart sank when he remembered that Connelly worked in the homicide division and two murders were committed in his living room less than 72 hours ago.

Before he had time to think his cell phone began to ring.

An unrecognized number popped up on the screen and he knew it was Biggs, very few people had his number and those that did were saved. Biggs never called him; all their business dealings took place in person, but since Khi had informed him that Jade was missing he had been calling him twice a day from different numbers to see if Khi had heard anything from her. Before he could answer the phone the bell rang again.

Ding Dong, Diiiinnnggg Dong, Ding Dong

"FUCCCCKKKKKKKKK" Khi said out loud, before declining the call, removing his gun from his waistline, and placing it inside his desk along with the phone.

He never saw the message that came through that read:

+407-859-9633

You have 24 hours to find her!

-B-

Khi inhaled and exhaled deeply before poising himself and heading to the door. He paused for a moment before opening it but knew that he didn't have a choice.

"Detective Connelly. How can I help you?" Khi said confidently. He didn't know what the fuck Connelly was doing at his door, but he wanted to be sure that nothing seemed suspicious.

"Good afternoon Mr. Banks, long time no see. Connelly replied smugly.

There was something about him that never sat right with Khi.

"Not long enough... You know considering your line of work, but once again how can I help you detective?" Khi asked quizzically.

"You can turn around and place your hands behind your back for me Mr. Banks. I have a warrant for your arrest!"

When Connelly announced the reason for his visit Khi lost all composure.

"What the fuck you mean you have a warrant for my arrest?" Khi yelled. This was the last thing he needed right now. His drug business was tight, they covered every base and were careful to never leave a trail. Unless there was a snitch in his Army, this wasn't drug related.

There was no way they had enough evidence to arrest him for Jade and Trinity's murders, he wasn't even the one that pulled the trigger. The Crew had gotten rid of the bodies and the weapons. None of this made any sense His mind immediately went to Rah.

This mutha fucka just shows up, my woman's gone and the Pigs at my door? Khi thought. Everything in him said that Rah was responsible until Connelly spoke again.

"You know I almost believed you that night when I took your statement. Who would have known that you killed your own god damn Mother!" Connelly Spat.

"The fuck you are talking about?" I didn't kill my mama nigga!" Khi snarled as the two uniformed officers attempted to apprehend him.

"Malachi Banks you are under arrest for the murder of Kathryn Banks. You have the right to remain silent..

Anything you say can and will be used against you in the court of law.. You have the right to an attorney, if you can't afford an attorney then one will be.....

"Fuck you! Fuck you Nigga!!" Khi yelled. Spit flew from his mouth as the officers cuffed him and escorted him to the police car. That moment was the straw that broke the camel's back. Kay had barely been back in his life for 6 months before he lost her again. He hadn't had time to truly mend their relationship or heal from losing her and now, he of all people was being charged with her murder!

He watched from the back seat of the Squad car as The Police put up the yellow tape officially making his home a murder scene.

▪▪▪

Rah frowned when he reached for Xanae and realized she wasn't there. The last two days they had spent together were perfect. They spent hours telling each other everything that had happened since he went to Jail. Neither of them held anything back. Xanae told him about Dame, Khi, Trinity, KJ and even Biggs and Cruz. She wanted the air to be clear.

Rah told her about life in prison, how he met Trinity and what he did for a living. Initially Xanae was taken back buy his line of work, but she didn't judge, he explained that after he lost KoKo and thought that Xanae was dead, he became numb. Nothing mattered, somehow vindicating those that felt they had been wronged made him feel as if he was getting his vengeance.

Xanae made it clear that she no longer wanted a life where she had to look over her shoulder or wonder if the man she loved was coming home at night. She wanted peace and if peace meant walking away from the Murder Game, then Rah was ready to throw in the towel. The feeling that Xanae gave him could never compare to any other. Relief washed over him when he realized she was in the kitchen. The smell of turkey bacon and waffles filled the cabin. Rah quickly got up, washed his face and brushed his teeth then made his way to the kitchen to greet Xanae.

"Good morning Beautiful" he said as he walked over and placed a kiss on her forehead.

"Good morning" Xanae smiled. She was smitten over him. Somehow everything she loved about him before he went to jail, she loved even more now that they had reconnected. When she was with him she felt safe, she felt heard and desired and loved. She couldn't deny that she was *in love* with Khi, but Rah was her person. She loved him from the depths of her soul, it wasn't a temporary emotion or something that would go away with time. They needed each other to feel whole. She didn't think that it was possible to love two people at once, but Khi and Rah had proved her wrong, although she was enjoying her time with Rah she couldn't help but think about how Khi was feeling. She had texted him the night before to let him know that she was safe and that they would talk soon and was surprised that he still hadn't responded. She figured that he needed time to process everything, and she was fine with that because honestly, she did too.

"Let me find out you learned how to cook while I was gone." Rah teased.

"Don't act like you forgot! Mama P taught me how to cook a long time ago. You definitely use to be begging me to Fry you some chicken every Friday night after the game."

"That's cause I liked you, Not the chicken" Rah shot back just before laughing and ducking an oven mitt that Xanae threw at him.

"Oh, so I guess that means you don't want any of this breakfast I made then huh?" Xanae said waving the plate filled with waffles, scrambled eggs, turkey bacon and fresh strawberries in front of him.

"Come on baby girl you know I'm just playing" Rah said as he instinctively grabbed her by her waist and pulled her closer to him.

They stared at each other for a split second before Xanae pulled away and tried to redirect the conversation. She placed the plate on the Dining room table and proceeded to the cabinet to look for a bottle of syrup. Rah responded by taking a seat in front of the food and thanking her. As much as he desired her, he didn't want to force anything, he wanted her to be comfortable with whatever happened next between them. "You know you didn't have to do this right?" Rah said as he grabbed the syrup from Xanae and poured it over his waffles. "I know I didn't, but I wanted to." Xanae replied as she took a sip of the hot chocolate she had made for herself.

"I gotta make some moves today, head to the city and get some things for the house. Do you wanna come with me?" Rah asked.

"Honestly I just want to relax today since we have a big day tomorrow." Xanae explained.

"A big day? It's your birthday or something?" Rah joked!

"Now don't pretend you don't know when my birthday is sir, because when it comes around, I want my gift!" Xanae joked back.

"I'll never forget your birthday Baby Girl, you know that, but whats up with tomorrow?"

"I talked to Mama P, I told her I was with you, and she misses you Rah! She needs us! Plus, I have to go pick up KJ. Her watching him for me while I'm going through all this mess has been a Godsend, but I can't put that burden on her for too long and I miss my baby so much. So, I told her that we would make the trip to North Carolina tomorrow, and she's expecting us bright and early."

Rah took a deep breath, rifling with his feelings. "I miss her too. I know that I should have gone to see her as soon as I got out, but it was just hard going back to that life once I found out about you and Koko." Rah explained sadly. "I understand, and she does too. I thought she was going to hate me when I showed up, but she was the same old Mama P. She embraced me, reassure me, fed me, took care of me like she always has since we were kids." Xanae replied.

"Well, how about this, I'll go get the stuff we need, when I get back I'll cook dinner since you made breakfast, and we will hit the road first thing tomorrow morning to head to Charlotte." "Cook? Ohh so now you a chef too?" Xanae laughed as she stole a piece of Turkey bacon off Rah's plate. She smiled as they talked, and he enjoyed his breakfast, but it was hard for her not to check her phone every 5 minutes to see if Khi had texted her back.

"Damn Nothing…. I'll give it time…" She thought

Chapter 24

Khi sat with his back against the wall staring at his cell mate. The frail black man with a salt and pepper beard and bald head had been referring to him as nephew since the moment he came. So far, the two had gotten along well but every moment that Khi spent behind bars felt like an eternity. He had been booked and processed but still hadn't spoken to his attorney or any members of his crew. He used his one phone call the first night he was booked to call Noriega. He needed any loose ends or possible evidence cleaned up, but Nori had missed the call. The next day he decided to call his Attorneys office instead. He hadn't spoken to his attorney directly, but his assistant informed Khi that Ms. Deveraux would meet with him today by 10:00

AM. Relief filled Khi when he finally heard the Guard call his name.

"Banks!! Your attorney is here, stand up and step away from the door." The officer commanded.

Khi followed his orders reluctantly. This was his first time ever being locked up and the one thing he wanted more than anything in the world was to walk out of that jail house free and clear.

The officer walked over to him and shackled his hands and feet together with handcuffs then led him to a visiting room where Danielle Deveraux sat waiting for him.

Danielle didn't look like your typical attorney, at first glance most would've mistaken her for a super model. She sat with her long legs crossed as she read her notes over her Prada frames. Her tan skin, full lips and thick hair that fell just below her breast gave her an exotic look, and her slanted eyes revealed hints of her asian heritage.

"Khi pulled away from the guard and took a seat in front of her on the other side of the table.

The guard started to react, but Danielle intervened.

"Thank you officer I'm sure Mr. Banks and I will be ok from here."

The guard smirked at Khi but backed away and stood in the corner, allowing the two to talk.

"Mr. Banks, you'll catch more bees with honey during your time here, don't get on the Guard's bad side. They will make it hard for you" Danielle warned.

"Fuck that shit Dani, my time here won't be long because I ain't do shit, post my bail and get me the fuck out of here today!" Khi barked.

"Khi it's not that simple. They have evidence against you and there is no bail. You have to see the Judge on Tuesday and then they will determine if you are eligible to be release on Bond!" Danielle explained.

"Tuesday? That's 3 days away Dani! How can they have evidence for some shit that I didn't do. My mama overdosed because she was a dope fiend! The needle killed her, and I couldn't do shit to save her! Khi replied hysterically.

"Khi there's a diary that your mother kept. I've asked for copies, but I haven't received them yet. The prosecutors are stating that there is a clear indication from your mother that you were trying to hurt her, and they have a motive."

Khi's gut clenched when he heard Danielle mention the journal. The same journal that Xanae told him about. The same journal that was missing.

"That doesn't make any sense. Why the fuck would I kill my mother?!" Khi questioned.

"Did you recently take out any insurance policies on your mother? Open any accounts for her? Any of that?" Danielle asked.

"Yeah, I opened an account for her, and I put money in it! A lot of money! She didn't even know how much was in there! So what?"

Mr. Banks, I don't have all the details yet, but so far, the prosecutors seem confident that there is a case here. For now, please be on your best behavior until I can get you out of here." Danielle said as she stood to leave.

Khi shook his head in defeat, he couldn't believe this was happening.

"Yo Dani, how did they get the journal?" Khi asked.

"An anonymous source dropped it off at the police station." Danielle said before disappearing from the room.

Anonymous source.... Anonymous source. Khi thought. He was trying so hard to put the pieces of the puzzle together that he didn't hear the guard telling him to stand up. A blow to the head sent him unconscious and when he woke up, he was in solitary confinement. He rubbed the back of his head and winced when he felt the small gash that had been left from the officer striking him. Damn it feel like this nigga hit me with a.........

Khi suddenly realized who took the journal to the police station.

"ROCK!!!!

FUCKING ROCK!!!!" Khi growled through gritted teeth.

STAY TUNED FOR FATAL FINESSE PART 3!!!

Made in the USA
Columbia, SC
25 April 2025

57153630R00226